CHOICES
A NOVEL

JUDITH BROWN

Lake Mary, Florida

Copyright © 1990 by Judith Brown
All rights reserved
Printed in the United States of America
Library of Congress Catalog Card Number: 89-82723
International Standard Book Number: 0-88419-270-9

Creation House
Strang Communications Company
600 Rinehart Road
Lake Mary, FL 32746
(407) 333-0600

This book or portions thereof may not be reproduced in any form without written permission of the publisher.

DEDICATION

For my granddaughter, Allison Leah Hartley

–ACKNOWLEDGMENTS–

I am grateful first to my family for their patience and perseverance which allowed me to try my hand at writing and ultimately to produce this manuscript. I am especially thankful to my husband, David, for his unwavering love, encouragement, support and prayerful guidance.

I appreciate the prayers and encouragement of my spiritual family—in particular, the group of women who read the original manuscript and bravely offered their suggestions. A special thanks goes to Pam Prag, a dear sister in the Lord and an intensive care nurse, who advised me on some of the technical aspects of the story.

I also want to thank Bob and Judy Mumford of Lifechangers for their encouragement and counsel. I owe a special debt of gratitude to Lloyd Hildebrand, who served as my agent; his practical advice and reassuring words kept me going through discouraging times.

Of course, I am indebted to Creation House for their publication of this manuscript and for giving me this opportunity. I am, indeed, privileged to work with them.

AUTHOR'S NOTE

I am forever impressed with our Father's unceasing efforts to draw us into the depths of understanding and compassion which were so exemplified in the life of our Savior. Since the first rendering of *Choices*, God has broadened my horizons through some of those difficult, painful life experiences one would opt to avoid if at all possible.

The past year has been filled with long hours in hospitals, a rehabilitation hospital and a nursing home, watching as a loved one battled with increasing debilitation—a profile of faith, courage and determination against mounting odds. Added to this was my own experience with major surgery and a period of hospitalization.

I have dedicated this book to my granddaughter, Allison Leah, who was born in a county where the number of births equals the number of abortions. She is one of the fortunate little ones whose mothers are not afraid of self-sacrifice. Still I don't want to overlook any of those who have put their own desires, hopes and dreams aside to care for another. There is no higher calling: Jesus is our example.

Many years ago a friend wrote a song which said that God would not move the mountains from our lives, but He would teach us how to climb them. I've never been able to forget that. As one who has led a moderately comfortable, blessed life, balanced with the painful lessons, I have found them to be faithful words.

This book, therefore, is for all those who are learning to climb the mountains in their own lives.

ONE

At first there were only muffled voices, like shapeless echoes. Then out of the mist one voice stirred memories of comfort and security. Could it be her mother's voice Margaret was hearing?

Mama, where are you? she called out in the darkness.

No response. Margaret tried to open her eyes, but without success. It was then she became aware of the terrible pain in her head. She wanted to cry out, but no sound came.

Now she could hear her father's voice. But hard as she tried, Margaret could not tell what they were saying. The only sound she understood was the crying.

Mama, please, don't cry. You know how upset it makes me. Why can't you hear me?

The pain was increasing, and the darkness soon engulfed her. Lost in space and time, Margaret drifted. Occasionally

CHOICES

the voices invaded her prison, always with unbearable pain, driving Margaret further into the silence and loneliness.

When the pain finally subsided, she strained toward the intruding sounds.

Where am I? What's happening to me?

Margaret felt a tug at her right eyelid. Then a blinding light—like an enormous floodlight—filled her vision. It went out as quickly as it came. She felt a tug at her left eyelid and braced herself. The light seared through her head like an explosion. The cooling darkness came, and her eyelid shut.

"Dr. Osborne, has there been any improvement?" Margaret heard her father ask.

Doctor? I must be in a hospital.

"I wish I could be more encouraging, Mr. Beaumont. But there doesn't seem to be any change in your daughter's condition whatsoever."

Margaret could hear her mother crying again.

"It's been over two weeks since the accident. Shouldn't there be some improvement by now?" her father asked.

Accident? Yes—I remember now. That car...coming toward me. Was it really two weeks ago?

The doctor spoke again. "As I told you before, the brain is a very complicated organ. Your daughter has suffered severe head trauma and cerebral hemorrhaging. The surgery stopped the bleeding, but there is no immediate way of determining the extent of damage, though her primary motor functions have been severely affected.

"The tests show compromised brain activity. Subsequent exams indicate a responsiveness to painful stimuli, and corneal reflexes are present."

"What does that mean in practical terms?" Paul Beaumont asked.

―――――――――――CHOICES―――――――――――

"It means," the doctor said, "that your daughter is paralyzed. She most likely will never recover. Her level of consciousness and comprehension is questionable, but we'll be able to assess that better as time goes on.

"She'll require total custodial care for an indefinite period of time. For now we can only try to keep her comfortable. I'm sorry, Mr. and Mrs. Beaumont. I'll keep you posted if there are any changes."

Paralyzed? The word hit Margaret like a bomb. *I can't be! She tried to move a hand, a toe, a finger—anything. Nothing.*

"Then she could be a...a vegetable?" Mrs. Beaumont asked.

The doctor didn't answer in words, but Margaret imagined him nodding.

I wish I could open my eyes and let them know I'm OK. Why can't I move?

The doctor was speaking again. Margaret listened intently.

"Have you made a decision yet concerning the pregnancy? I must remind you that the longer you wait, the harder and more dangerous it will be."

I'm still pregnant!

There was a long silence. Finally Margaret's mother spoke.

"We've thought about it very carefully and have decided against the abortion. We won't be responsible for the death of our own grandchild. I'm certain our Margaret would want it that way."

Oh, Mother, that's crazy! Let them end the pregnancy! You can't expect me to carry a baby in this condition.

"Mrs. Beaumont," the doctor said, "I think we need to look at the facts here. Your daughter is in critical condition and in her third month of pregnancy. She would have to go at least another four or five months for the fetus to have any

9

chance at all. We cannot tell what effect the pregnancy will have on Margaret's chances for survival or what effects the trauma of the accident and the many drugs used in her treatment will have on the fetus. I should inform you too that Margaret had an appointment for an abortion on the morning of the accident. She apparently had made her decision."

Mrs. Beaumont was crying again. "I can't believe it! Margaret isn't that kind of girl!"

Be real, Mother! You have no idea what kind of girl I am.

TWO

The colors of autumn were just beginning to show as Margaret pulled into her parking space. She breathed in the fresh morning air, enjoying the chrysanthemums landscaped in neat rows around the entrance to the building.

Harold Jenkins, the branch manager, was in front of her. He held the door open.

"Good morning, Margaret," he said. "Did you have a good weekend?"

"Yes, thank you. I took Friday off and spent it with my folks. Their complaints of neglect finally got to me."

Jenkins chuckled. "I guess I have to take your parents' side. I can never get enough of my children or my grandchildren."

They paused outside the door to Margaret's department.

"Margaret, as soon as you can, I'd like you to drop by my office."

"Certainly. I'll check my messages and be right in."

Margaret's heart was beating rapidly as she opened the door and walked down the corridor between the two rows of cubicles.

"Good morning, Margaret," a tall, red-haired woman in the cubicle opposite hers called out.

"Hi, Annie." Margaret placed her briefcase and purse on her desk.

Annie stepped across the hall. "Mr. Jenkins was looking for you Friday," she said. "Maybe it's about your promotion."

"I just ran into him. He told me to come to his office right away. I guess we'll know soon."

"I hope you get it. You've certainly worked hard enough. If anyone deserves it, you do."

"Thanks for the vote of confidence. But I'm not sure. My age could pose a problem. I don't know of too many twenty-eight-year-old assistant managers in this organization. They're more likely to transfer someone in from another office."

"Well, I'll keep my fingers crossed anyway."

"Thanks."

Margaret arranged the pile of messages on her desk, made a few notations and headed off down the hall.

"Miss Beaumont is here, Mr. Jenkins," the plump, white-haired secretary announced.

"Send her in."

Harold Jenkins's office was comfortable but not impressive

by most corporate standards. He was a practical man with simple tastes. The paneled walls were bare except for a few plaques and some pictures of him receiving various awards. Photographs of his wife and family adorned the credenza in back of the desk.

Margaret liked Jenkins. He was one of those rare individuals who could hold your respect with his professional manner without diminishing his humanity. Today, however, Margaret was uneasy.

"I'm sure you can guess the reason for this talk," Jenkins said.

"I assume it's about my request for a promotion."

Jenkins smiled and brushed his hand over his balding head. "Yes. Well, I won't keep you in suspense. The home office is very impressed with your work. They've authorized me to offer you the position of assistant manager for this office. Congratulations."

Margaret sighed with relief, then grasped Jenkins's outstretched hand.

"Thank you. Thank you very much. I'm really honored. When do I start?"

"Gillespie will be transferring to the Buffalo office at the beginning of the month. As soon as you can get free of your own accounts, I want you to get together with him. He'll acquaint you with your new duties before he leaves. You'll also need to spend next week at the home office for training. Plan to arrive Sunday evening and return Saturday. I'll have my secretary make the arrangements for you."

Annie was waiting as Margaret returned to their department.

"Well?"

"I got it, Annie! Meet your new boss!"

"Oh, Margaret, that's wonderful!" Annie hugged her. "When can I put in for a raise?"

Margaret laughed. "I don't know about that. But how about celebrating over lunch? My treat."

Annie's smile faded. "I'd love to, Margaret, but it's Monday, you know—my day to picket. How about tomorrow?"

"It wouldn't be the same. Can't you miss picketing just this once?"

"I really can't. It's a commitment. They count on me."

Margaret continued down the corridor. "Do you really think it does any good?"

Annie stood in the cubicle entrance. "It keeps the issue of abortion before the public. That's worthwhile."

Margaret sat down at her desk and eyed Annie. "But why you?"

"I'm adopted."

"So? What does that have to do with it?"

"If abortion had been legal when I was born, I'm sure my natural mother would have taken that option. I'm happy to be alive, and I'd like to see all those unwanted babies have the same chance I had."

"I guess I haven't thought much about it."

Margaret knew Annie wanted to pursue the subject further, but abortion wasn't exactly the hot topic on her mind right then.

"Well, I guess I better get to work," Margaret said. "We'll plan lunch for tomorrow."

"Good. I promise I'll be just as excited for you tomorrow."

——————CHOICES——————

Margaret watched Annie return to her cubicle, resolving not to bring up the subject again.

The first day at corporate headquarters was draining. In fact, Margaret was downright bored. But the second day held greater promise.

As she entered the elevator, a man joined her. Margaret recognized him immediately: John Farnham, the vice president in charge of sales. He had visited Margaret's branch several times.

"Good morning, Mr. Farnham."

A brief silence followed Margaret's greeting. The questioning look on the man's face gave way to a polite smile. "Are you new with the company?" he asked.

"No, sir. But I'm not with the home office, either. I've just been promoted to assistant branch manager, and I'm here for training."

"Oh, yes, Miss—"

"Beaumont. Margaret Beaumont."

Farnham studied her quietly for another moment. The elevator door opened, and Margaret stepped out.

"Have a good day, Mr. Farnham."

"Yes, you too, Miss Beaumont." As the elevator door was closing, Farnham jumped forward, pushed the hold button and stopped the door. "Being new to the area, you're probably hard-pressed to know what to do with your evenings."

"I guess you could say that."

"Well, I'm giving a small party at my home this evening in honor of a foreign buyer. I'd be pleased if you could come. It would give you a chance to mingle with the company

15

executives in a more casual setting."

The invitation surprised Margaret. She hesitated.

"You'd be a delightful addition to the evening," Farnham said.

"Thank you. I'd love to come."

"Good. I'll have my secretary get in touch with you sometime this morning to give you the details."

He released the door, and it closed.

Ah! Annie and the others would be so jealous! she chuckled to herself. They can hardly keep their eyes off him whenever he comes to our office.

Although in his late forties, Farnham looked younger—tall, trim and dashing. The only evidence of his age was the striking gray hair at his temples.

But why me? Why did he invite *me* to his party?

She knew all the top management would be there. Here was her opportunity to shine! In that moment she felt as though nothing could stop her climb up the ladder to success.

Margaret hurried down the hall to her training session in the accounting department.

THREE

MARGARET HAD THOUGHT OF EVERYthing when she packed, even her most elegant party dress—royal blue with a plunging back. The dress accented her striking blue eyes and her trim figure.

"It's perfect!" She checked out her reflection in the mirror. "I'm pretty dazzling after all!"

She added a single strand of pearls with gold beads and a matching pair of dangling earrings. Cascades of blonde curls framed her face.

Entering the gate to the long, circular driveway, Margaret couldn't help but feel she had "arrived."

Her host's residence was a large, brick house with a columned portico. Although not quite a mansion, it was breathtaking.

The hostess was a handsome woman who appeared to be

much older than her husband. She was well-dressed, but obviously losing her battle with age. Margaret couldn't help but think how mismatched they seemed.

She greeted her host and hostess and moved into the great room to mingle with the other guests. On several occasions she looked up to see John Farnham staring at her from across the room.

Later in the evening he met her in the hallway as she returned from the powder room.

"I hope you're enjoying yourself," he said.

"Very much, Mr. Farnham."

"John, please. Call me John."

"If you like—uhh—John."

"I'm glad this little party coincided with your visit to headquarters. I've been impressed with your work and have been eager to meet you. Congratulations on your promotion."

"Why, thank you, John."

"I hope you won't think me forward, but I must say I never expected you to be so beautiful. It isn't noted anywhere in your file. I'm not sure what I was expecting, but you certainly surpass anything I could have imagined."

A warm flush spread over Margaret's cheeks. He *was* being forward. But it felt good.

"Say, have you met my father-in-law yet?" he asked.

"Your father-in-law?"

"Yes, Simon P. Minton."

"The president of the company is your father-in-law?" she asked, her blue eyes wide. "No, I haven't met him."

"Come on. I'll introduce you."

John Farnham had no sooner completed the introduction when his wife called to him to join her. He excused himself, promising to talk with her later.

But not until Margaret was leaving did they encounter each other again.

"Thank you so much for inviting me," she said. "I had a wonderful time. Now I can place the faces of all the signatures that have crossed my desk over the past five years."

"Thank you for coming," Farnham smiled. "As far as I'm concerned, you made the party."

Margaret blushed in spite of herself. "Well, I better get back to the hotel and get some rest," she said. "I don't want to be late to the office."

"You wouldn't mind adding another item to your already busy schedule, would you? A business luncheon with a company vice president?"

"That would be lovely. Thank you."

"Good," John said. "Drop by my office around noon."

"See you then," she said, smiling as she moved toward the door.

Driving back to her hotel, Margaret was under no delusions about John Farnham's intentions. Still, she wasn't the least bit uncomfortable. In fact, she was flattered by the attentions of this powerful, appealing man. It was all part of the game.

John took Margaret to his club for lunch. It was in an old brownstone, very posh.

After placing their order, John sat back and studied his companion.

"No doubt you're the fairest creature ever to grace these sacred halls," he said. "In fact, up until six months ago women weren't even allowed in here."

"I guess this club was a little slower than most to see the

light," Margaret said over her glass of wine.

John laughed. "It was hard on some of the older members —a few of them resigned in protest. We've more than made up for them, though, with all the businesswomen who stormed the gates when our change of policy was announced."

"You don't mind the change then?"

"Not really, though there is a part of me that mourns the loss of deep-rooted tradition."

Margaret glanced at a nearby table where two attractive, well-dressed women sat. "No place for the poor little rich boys to hide anymore, is there?"

"I'm afraid not. I guess it doesn't bother me so much because I haven't been a 'poor little rich boy' all my life. I didn't inherit my membership here, as many of the others did."

"Really?"

"Would you believe my father worked on an auto assembly line in Detroit?"

"You've come a long way then."

"I was luckier than most, I guess. Most of my high school buddies are still back home eking out a living in the same factories where their fathers worked."

"What made the difference?"

John sipped his wine. "I won a substantial college scholarship and happened to choose the right school. That's where I met Virginia. She changed my entire financial situation the moment I married her."

Margaret looked at him suspiciously.

"No, no," John said, "I didn't marry her for her money. I really did love her...then."

"And now?"

"I still love her in a way. We've grown apart over the years. I travel a lot, and I have my business relationships.

She's involved with the kids and her charities. Except for an occasional social event, she goes her way and I go mine. I decided a long time ago that I'd see the marriage through. At first it was for the kids' sake. But now that they're older, it's mostly because I don't want to upset the apple cart."

Margaret understood exactly what he meant. Any serious problems in the marriage could make Simon P. Minton unhappy and jeopardize John's career.

The waiter placed a steaming bowl of cream of broccoli soup in front of each of them.

"Enough about me," John said. "Now it's your turn. Who is Margaret Beaumont?"

Margaret put her spoon down and sat back. "Well, I guess Margaret Beaumont is a small-town girl who moved to the big city to seek her fortune. I was brought up in a farming community in upstate New York. The Beaumonts were one of the earliest families in the area and still hold a good percentage of the property in town. My father, and his father before him, ran the local drugstore."

"So you're one of those 'poor little rich girls,' are you?"

"I honestly don't know," Margaret said. "We never wanted for anything, but my father was always careful with money. At least until he saw someone in need. Then he was generous. When my mother would complain about his generosity, he'd become very annoyed."

Margaret cleared her throat and, in a husky voice, intoned, " 'The good Lord has found He can trust us to disperse His goods wisely, and I wouldn't want to cut off the flow and cause them to back up. Who knows, maybe God would look down from heaven, figure we had enough and not send us anymore.' "

John laughed, and Margaret joined him.

"So your father's a religious man?" John asked.

"Very. He tried to be strict with us kids. But usually my mother intervened—most often on my behalf. Mom was—and still is, for that matter—the family peacemaker."

Margaret paused to take more of her soup.

"Brothers or sisters?" John asked.

"Oh, yes, two. Tom is ten years older than I am. He left for college when I was seven so we were never close. I don't think he ever did anything wrong in his life. Maybe he was so much older that I wasn't aware of his problems. But I only remember the awards he brought home. He became a doctor, married a nurse and went off to New Guinea as a medical missionary."

"Sounds like a hard act to follow."

"I think it was probably harder on my sister than me. She was four years behind him and was forever struggling with what everyone else expected of her. Then I came along and knocked her off her pedestal. I think she's spent the rest of her life getting back at me. Anyway, she went into teaching but only stayed at it for two years before she married. Her husband has had moderate success in politics. You'd think he'd been elected president to hear Jessica talk."

John pulled closer to the table and leaned on his elbows. "Any—what do they say today—'significant others' in the picture?"

Margaret finished her soup before she replied.

"No. There was someone until six months ago. He was transferred to California. I wasn't about to give up my career to go with him, so we called it quits."

The conversation turned to lighter subjects as the main course was brought, but when the coffee was served John became serious again.

"Margaret, I've really enjoyed having lunch with you. I wish we could spend more time together while you're here, but I'm scheduled to leave on a business trip at 6:30 in the morning. I, uhh...I was wondering if you'd be open to having dinner with me the next time I visit your office."

Margaret's cheeks were flushed. "Well, I guess I'd consider it."

"We'd have to keep it quiet, of course."

"I understand. My lips are sealed."

John smiled warmly.

Margaret was home from headquarters only a few minutes when her apartment doorbell rang. She opened the door to find a man holding a box of long-stemmed red roses. She took them inside and read the card. "To the loveliest assistant manager in the company, from her Number 1 admirer."

Almost a month had passed when Jenkins informed Margaret that Farnham planned to visit at the end of the week.

Where can this relationship possibly go? He *is* a married man, after all. But she counted the days on her calendar.

When the telephone rang later that evening, she took a deep breath before answering.

"Hello, Margaret."

"Oh...John? Hello."

"Did you hear that I'm coming to your office this week?"

"Yes, Mr. Jenkins mentioned it today."

"Have you thought about my invitation to dinner?"

Margaret's hand tightened on the receiver.

"John, I don't know. What about your wife?"

"She won't know. Margaret, I've been looking forward to seeing you. Please don't disappoint me."

Her heart skipped a beat. One voice cried, "Yes!" Another voice whispered, "But he's married."

"I'd love to go," she finally blurted.

"Wonderful! Meet me at my hotel Friday night at 7:00. We'll have dinner and see what the evening brings."

"OK, I'll be there."

"I can't wait!"

"Neither can I."

"Good morning, Annie," Margaret said, as she joined her friend at the door of the office building two mornings later.

"Hi, Margaret." Annie held the door open. "No doubt we'll have 100 percent attendance today—at least as far as the women go."

Margaret stopped in the entrance. "Why do you say that?"

"Well, word got around that John Farnham's going to be here today."

"I know the girls swoon over him, but I didn't think he affected them that much."

"Well, just don't expect too much work from them today, boss."

Annie winked at Margaret and entered her department. Margaret continued down the corridor to her new office. Her secretary hadn't arrived yet. She glanced at herself one last time in the mirror and sat down at her desk. She took a folder from the desktop organizer and opened it. Only moments later she closed it.

This is ridiculous! I'm acting like a lovesick school girl. Grow up, Margaret!

Just then she heard a knock. She looked up to see John standing in the doorway.

"May I come in, Miss Beaumont?" he asked.

"Why certainly, Mr. Farnham." Margaret stood and

stretched out her hand. "So nice to see you again."

John took her hand and kissed it instead of shaking it. "Even lovelier than I remembered," he said.

"John, please," she said in hushed tones. "My secretary will be coming any minute."

John released her hand and took a seat. "I went to Jenkins's office first, but he wasn't in yet. So I thought I'd see if the assistant manager was."

"Oh, there you are, John," Jenkins said, stepping into the office. "I thought I saw you coming in the building as I drove up."

The two men shook hands.

"My plane got in a little earlier than I had expected," John said.

"Well, come into my office. I'll have my secretary get us some coffee while I update you. Margaret, you can join us when you have time."

Margaret nodded, then picked up the folder again, her eyes trying to focus on the printed words. Twenty minutes later she was seated in the extra chair in Jenkins's office.

That evening Margaret pulled into the hotel parking lot at exactly 7:00. She was dressed in a black satin-and-lace suit. Rhinestone earrings glittered against her blonde curls.

She sat in the car a while, hoping five or ten minutes more would conceal her eagerness. She finally got out. A brisk October breeze blew across the parking lot, ruffling her hair and chilling her.

John was waiting in the lobby. He opened the door with a flourish before her hand could reach it.

"Brrrr," she said. "I guess I'm going to have to accept

it that summer's gone and wear a coat."

"It might help. But then you'd take away my excuse to put my arm around you to warm you up."

Margaret glanced down coyly, not wanting her eyes to give away her excitement.

John guided her to the dining room. After dinner, they found a corner table in the lounge. They were barely settled in their seats when the band struck up a fast dance tune.

"May I?" John asked with mock formality.

"Ooh, Mr. Farnham," she said, smiling and taking his proffered hand. "I didn't know you had it in you!"

"Hey, don't underestimate me. I can still cut the rug when I want to."

Once on the dance floor, he whirled her and swung her until they both laughed with pleasure. Their mood easily followed the lead of music when a slow-dance number filled the room.

John gazed into her eyes and pulled her to him, his cheek pressing against hers.

Am I crazy? she thought, her pulse pounding in her ears. This could easily get out of hand!

There were drinks, more dances and conversation with their heads so close together she could feel his warm breath in her ear.

Margaret's head buzzed. She knew she had had too much to drink, but the pleasure of being held so close to John blurred her thoughts. His kisses added to the intoxication that was overtaking her. Much later, Margaret followed John to his suite.

She awoke with a start. A few rays of morning sun filtered in around the edges of the drapes—enough for her to make out her surroundings. She wasn't alone. Hazy memories of the night before came back to her. Her head ached.

This isn't right, she chastised herself. Yes, I did live with a man for almost two years. But that was different. I'm not the type for a one-night stand with a married man.

She slipped out of bed and tiptoed into the bathroom. John stirred, then quieted again.

Margaret got dressed and came out of the bathroom. Just then John woke up.

"Come here, Margaret," he said.

"I think I'd better be going, John."

He put out his hand to her. "Why? It's Saturday. You don't have to work, and I don't have to catch my plane until 2:30."

"I'm sorry, but I really have to go."

"When can I see you again?"

"The next time business requires it," she said, not meeting his eyes.

John put his hand down. "I'm not talking about business."

Margaret let out a deep sigh. "I'm sorry, John. This just isn't for me. I thought I could handle it, but I can't." She backed away.

"OK, OK," John said quickly. "Just don't make your mind up too fast. I'll give you a call the next time I'm in town."

Margaret didn't answer. She let herself out.

Forget it ever happened, she told herself.

She got in her car and drove away.

FOUR

It was just beginning to snow as Margaret arrived at her parents' old Victorian house. Two wreaths hung on the double front door, and electric candles twinkled from the windows. Only the Christmas tree was missing. That would be placed in the large downstairs bay window after dinner.

The familiar aromas of Evelyn Beaumont's Christmas cookies and fruitcakes greeted Margaret as she opened the back door.

"Anybody home?" she called.

Mrs. Beaumont rushed from the dining room. "Oh, Margaret! We weren't expecting you for another hour or so."

The two women hugged.

"I got started earlier than I expected. Where is everyone?"

"Your father's still at the store, and Jessica hasn't arrived yet. The others are scattered around the house."

Mrs. Beaumont moved toward the hallway and called out, "Margaret's here!"

Margaret's brother, Tom, and his wife, Sally, came down the stairs. Their two children, Elizabeth and Elias, ran in from the living room.

"Look at these two!" Margaret said. "I realize just how long three years is when I see how much they've grown."

"It's good to see you again, sis," Tom said, giving her a bear hug. "You look terrific!"

Sally hugged Margaret warmly. "We heard about your promotion. Maybe with a bigger salary and a longer vacation, you'll be able to come and see us."

"Hmmm," Margaret replied, "I'll consider it. But right now I have a much shorter trip in mind than to New Guinea. You two men come with me. There's a lot to bring in from the car."

Just as the last of the packages was taken out of the trunk, Margaret's sister, Jessica, and her husband, Hugh, pulled into the driveway. Their three little ones, Chenelle, Adrianna and Theodore, burst out of the car even before their father had turned off the engine.

"Hello, Margaret, dear," Jessica said as the two embraced stiffly. "You can't imagine how glad I am to get out of that car. Next time we fly!"

"It's certainly the best way," Margaret said quickly. "Here, let me help you." She reached behind her sister for some of the brightly wrapped gifts and carried them inside.

Within an hour they were all eating the Beaumont family's traditional Christmas Eve dinner of chicken and dumplings.

"So, Tom, how are things in the jungle?" Jessica asked.

Tom looked up from his plate and shook his head. "Jessica, you know we don't live in the jungle. We live in the city and enjoy many of the same conveniences you do."

"I know you've told me that. But I can't help but picture a thatched-roof hut off in the jungles somewhere."

"I do go into the interior on a regular basis," Tom said. "But we don't live there."

Jessica was silent for a short time, then continued. "Margaret, you must have some opinion about your brother spending so much time out of the country."

"Actually I have no opinion at all about it. He can do what he wants with his life. He's a grown man and quite capable of making his own decisions."

"Gee, thanks for the rousing vote of confidence, sis," Tom said.

"I just don't think it's right to go traipsing off to some Third World country, dragging the children behind," Jessica said.

"Well, Jessica, I can appreciate your concerns, but Sally and I believe it's a positive experience for our children," Tom said. "How many children have the rich cross-cultural experience ours do? Elizabeth and Elias have seen with their own eyes what other American children only read about."

"Pass the dumplings, please," Paul Beaumont interrupted.

Jessica handed her father the bowl heaped with dumplings and continued the conversation. "I can't help but wonder what kind of Americans they're going to be, anyway—I mean, spending so little time in the United States and all."

Tom's patience was wearing thin. "I think they'll make good citizens," he said. "I would hope they'd be able to see their country from a clearer perspective than most. Perhaps see it as it really is—as part of the world community. I hope they'll discern accurately what's right and what's wrong with their country. Beyond that, I hope they'll see

―――――――――――― CHOICES ――――――――――――

the kingdom of God above the kingdoms of men."

"Oh, honestly, Tom, you always revert to your idyllic fantasies of heaven on earth. At least Margaret has something to show for her years of work."

Sally had had enough. "Jessica, why do you have to hammer away at this point every time we get together? Have we ever accused you of child neglect for the long periods of time you're away from home with Hugh on his campaigns? At least our children are with us."

"Now that's enough!" Evelyn Beaumont said. "I refuse to sit here and listen to you criticize each other. You're all doing what you feel is best in your particular situations, and I'm equally proud of all of you."

"Your mother's right," Paul said. "Let's end this argument, or whatever it is, right now."

Evelyn started to clean off the table. "I don't want any more disagreements or complaints while you're in this house. This is supposed to be a time to enjoy one another. It's Christmas, and I'm just happy my family's all together."

Paul rose to his feet. "OK, men. While the women are cleaning up, we better get busy on the tree. We don't want to be late for the candlelight service."

Margaret knew there would be no more quarreling in her mother's presence. But she still anticipated the inevitable confrontation over her single status. It finally came the day after Christmas.

Margaret got up that morning not feeling too well. She took a shower but returned to her room to lie down. She had been nauseated on and off for more than a month. By now she was pretty sure why. It was no stomach virus. She could no longer deny the possibility that she was pregnant.

As she lay on her bed, a knock came at the door.

"Margaret, it's Jessica. May I come in?"

32

Everything within her wanted to yell, Go away!

"Sure, come on in," she said instead. She sat up and tried to be pleasant.

"Mom wants to know when you're coming down for breakfast."

"I'm not in much of a mood to eat anything. I think I ate too much yesterday—my stomach is pretty upset."

"You don't look well. Maybe I should get Tom."

"No, no, don't do that. There's no need to bother him over a simple case of overeating."

"Well, at least let me get you a cup of tea."

Jessica was gone before Margaret could respond. Whether she wanted a cup of tea or not, it looked as though she was going to get one. She fluffed the pillows in back of her and sat up.

A few minutes later Jessica returned, carrying the steaming cup. "This should help," she said.

"Thanks. I'm sure it's just what I need."

Jessica handed her sister the cup and sat down on the edge of the bed.

Margaret took a sip of the tea, put it back on the saucer, and said, "OK, Jessica, what's on your mind?"

"Is it that obvious?"

"Yes."

"Well, I guess I have to say I was really disappointed when I heard you broke up with that Charles. I never did meet him, but from everything I heard about him, I thought for sure you'd get married. I mean, you dated him for over two years. What happened?"

"It was a simple matter of a transfer—he had to move to California, and I didn't want to go."

Jessica's mouth dropped open. "You broke up because of *that?* You're crazy for not going with him."

CHOICES

"I couldn't drop *my* career just to tag along with him."

"Really, Margaret, it's about time you settled down and started to think about a family. You wait much longer, and it'll be too late. You're not getting any younger, you know. Besides, it would make Mom so happy."

"Never mind what *I* want or what makes *me* happy, eh?"

"Of course I care about what makes you happy. I just don't want to see life pass you by. Sure, you have a nice car, expensive clothes, money in the bank—but you're missing the really important things in life."

Margaret took another sip of tea and shook her head. "Jessica, I appreciate your concern. But obviously we don't see eye to eye about how I should live my life. As I told you last year, and the year before that, I'm just not ready to quit my job to spend my days cleaning house and changing diapers. And your hounding me on the subject isn't helping one bit, either!"

"Well, I guess you have to do what you have to do," said Jessica, smoothing the comforter and smiling artificially. "I just hope you're not going to regret it."

She left the room, closing the door behind her.

Margaret put the cup and saucer on the nightstand a little too loudly. Who does she think she is, anyway? She placed her hands on her abdomen. Tears clouded her eyes as the reality of her condition struck her.

Dear God, I'm definitely not ready for a child. I've got to make an appointment at the clinic as soon as I get back.

"The doctor will see you now, Miss Beaumont," the receptionist said. "Her office is the fourth door on the left."

"Thank you," Margaret said.

―――――――― CHOICES ――――――――

Her legs were shaky as she started down the hall. The office door was open.

"Come right in," the doctor said.

The doctor was an attractive middle-aged woman. She was small in stature and had dark hair streaked with gray. She exuded both confidence and warmth. Margaret felt comfortable with her from the first moment she had met her in the examination room.

Margaret took a seat across the desk. She wrung her perspiring hands as she awaited the results of the tests and examination.

"Well, it seems the evidence confirms your suspicions," the doctor said. "You are between ten and twelve weeks' pregnant."

At first Margaret did not respond. A numbness washed over her body. Then, suddenly, the dam that had been holding back her emotions gave way in a stream of tears. The doctor left her chair and moved to her patient's side.

"Margaret, I know it seems like an impossible situation right now, but you'll get through it," the doctor said.

"I feel so foolish. I knew I was pregnant. But hearing you say it wipes out the last hope that I might have been wrong."

Margaret was crying again.

"You're not foolish. It's perfectly normal to cry in your circumstances."

"What...what am I going to do? I can't have this baby!"

The doctor stood up and handed Margaret a box of tissues.

When Margaret had gotten her emotions back under control, the doctor returned to her desk.

"It's only natural for you to feel overwhelmed right now, but in a few days things will be a little clearer. You just have to find the plan which is best for you. There are a number of options—including the termination of the

35

pregnancy should you decide not to go to term."

"Can I make an appointment right now for an abortion?"

"Yes, you could...but wouldn't you like to take some time? Think about it when you're not so emotional? It won't make any difference if the procedure is done tomorrow or four or five days from now."

Margaret hesitated. "I guess this is something I shouldn't rush into—not that waiting a few days is going to change my mind."

"I'll give you some information, and as soon as you make up your mind, you can call for an appointment."

Margaret went to the ladies' room and freshened her makeup before leaving the clinic. She was expected back at work after lunch. It was a little past noon. Maybe after a bite to eat she'd be ready to face the office.

She opened the front door and stepped out onto the sidewalk. Several picketers were carrying their graphic signs.

"Margaret?" one of the protesters said.

Margaret looked in the direction of the voice. It was Annie. Oh, no! It's Monday!

She turned and hurried down the sidewalk, pretending she hadn't seen her co-worker. Annie handed her sign to one of her companions and followed after her.

"Margaret, are you all right?" she asked.

"I'm fine!"

"I just want to be of help if you have a problem.

Margaret stopped and faced Annie.

"I told you I'm fine. Please just let me be."

"Margaret, we've been friends a long time. I can tell by your expression you weren't in there just to get birth control pills."

"Look, Annie, I appreciate your wanting to help, but I'm

CHOICES

afraid you'd just confuse me further. The only thing you can do for me is to forget you ever saw me coming out that door."

Annie put a reassuring hand on Margaret's arm.

"I know people who can help you. It'll all be confidential. Please, give your baby a chance at life."

Margaret pulled her arm away. "I'll say it once more—I don't want your help! Now leave me alone!"

Annie watched with tears in her eyes as Margaret turned away sharply.

Three times Margaret had picked up the phone and returned it to its cradle without dialing. Now she picked it up for the fourth time, cleared her throat and dialed. She was about to hang up after the fifth ring when she heard a woman's voice.

"Hello?"

"Uhh...Mrs. Farnham?"

"Yes."

"My name is Margaret Beaumont. I'm an assistant manager in the company. I'm really sorry to bother Mr. Farnham at home, but something's come up at the office that needs to be handled with the utmost confidentiality. I didn't feel comfortable calling him at the office. Would it be possible to speak with him?"

"Ahhh...yes. Just a moment."

It seemed like an eternity to Margaret as she waited for John to come to the phone. Finally she heard him pick it up, and the other phone click as it was returned to its cradle.

"Miss Beaumont, this is...rather unusual," John said.

Margaret could hear a sound like a door closing.

"What on earth are you doing, calling me at home?" he whispered.

"I'm sorry, John, but I just had to talk with you."

"How am I going to explain this to my wife?"

"I already took care of that. I told her I was calling about a confidential matter at the office. All you have to do is tell her that I found some irregularities in the books and was concerned."

"Great! And what if word about *that* gets around?"

"I don't know! Tell her I made a mistake, and you were able to clear up the misunderstanding or something."

"So what's so important that you would risk calling me?"

Margaret could feel tears welling up in her eyes. "John, I'm pregnant."

There was a long silence.

"Are you still there?" Margaret asked.

"Yes, I'm still here." His voice was cold. "Why are you calling me?"

Margaret swallowed hard and wiped a tear from her cheek. "You're the father."

"How do I know that?"

Margaret was stunned. "You're the only one it could possibly be."

"Look, Margaret, I know you're probably pretty desperate right now, but that's no reason to implicate me."

"John, what are you talking about? What do you mean, 'implicate' you? You're the baby's father. I just thought I should talk with you before I made the final decision."

"You are going to have an abortion, aren't you? I'm certainly in no position to raise the child, and I don't want some stranger knocking on my door twenty years from now, demanding his share of my money."

Margaret was sobbing. She hadn't expected such callousness.

John spoke again. This time his voice was gentler. "I'm

sorry. I guess I've been rather harsh. It's just that this comes as such a shock. I thought a woman of your position would take precautions.''

He sighed. ''Look, I can imagine it's been difficult for you, but you know I can't take any responsibility in the situation. The only thing I can do is send you some money to help you out of this. Do whatever you have to do, but I do think an abortion is probably the best thing.''

''I don't want your money. I guess I just wanted to know you were in agreement about the abortion.''

''Well, I am. Whether you want the money or not, I'm going to send it. It's the least I can do.''

''Thank you, but it's really not necessary.''

''Listen, I've got to go. Take care of yourself. I hope all goes well with you.''

''Good-bye, John.''

Margaret hung up the phone and sat quietly for a while. She would call the clinic in the morning.

It's just fetal tissue, Margaret told herself, her thoughts warring with everything she'd been brought up to believe. It doesn't even look like a baby yet.

FIVE

THE ALARM BUZZED AT 6:30. MARGARET pulled the pillow over her head to shut out the intruding noise, but in vain. She finally yielded to the alarm clock and got out of bed.

She stumbled into the bathroom and showered. Next stop was the kitchen, where she brewed a pot of coffee, then the front door to get the newspaper. She returned to the kitchen and threw an English muffin in the toaster oven. Numbness swept over her, and her normal morning routine came to an abrupt end.

She retrieved the English muffin, burning her fingers.

"Drat! I'm not supposed to eat anything."

She poured the coffee down the drain, savoring the aroma. Sighing, she sat down at the table and read the newspaper, trying not to think. She left the kitchen and headed for the bedroom, straightening up the magazines and sofa cushions as she went. She knew she wouldn't be feeling up to housework when she returned.

It was time to get dressed. She passed over her gray suit and pink silk blouse and chose instead a pair of jeans and a loose sweater. She wanted to be comfortable.

Picking up her purse, she left the apartment and rode the elevator to the parking garage. For a moment her emotions flared, and she steeled herself against the rush of guilt. By the time she reached her car, she was in control again.

There is absolutely no reason for me to be nervous. Millions of women have gone through this. Soon I'll be free of this...this inconvenience. A few hours from now it'll all be behind me.

Her nervous fingers fumbled to get the key in the ignition. The key dropped to the floor. She felt around with her hand. No use. Finally, she let loose a barrage of four-letter words, shocking even herself.

Calm down.

She stepped out of the car to look for the key. Finding it caught on the edge of the mat, she returned to her seat and backed out of the space, then started up the ramp to street level. The early morning fog still blanketed the city.

She hoped her mother and father would never find out—they were staunch anti-abortionists. They would say she was killing their grandchild, even if it was illegitimate.

Annie's face flashed before her. Her words rang in Margaret's ears: "Please, give your baby a chance at life."

Margaret's eyes filled with tears, blurring her vision in the morning mist as she pulled into traffic. In a flash Margaret Beaumont's plans were changed, not just for this day, but for the rest of her life.

She spotted the car a split second before impact and

swerved. The sound of screeching brakes, grinding metal and shattering glass filled her ears. Then silence...and a consuming darkness.

The next thing Margaret knew, someone was bending over her, tugging at her seatbelt. Her eyes opened, but her vision was blurred, and an excruciating pain pierced her head. Something warm trickled down her face.

"Take it easy, miss," her rescuer said. "I'll have you out of here in no time."

The man shifted his position to get at the seatbelt from another angle.

Margaret smelled gasoline. She panicked. The stranger wasn't able to release the seatbelt, either.

Get me out of here before this thing blows up! She tried to scream, but no sound came out. She made a desperate effort to reach out toward the man, but her arms wouldn't move.

Get me out of here! Get me out of here!

The rescuer backed out of the passenger's side. "I can't get the seatbelt off," Margaret heard him say. "Get me something to cut it with. Hurry!"

Although it seemed like an eternity to Margaret, it was only a matter of seconds before the stranger was back. She couldn't see what he was using to cut through the seatbelt, but she could feel him working at it. Finally it snapped. He quickly got rid of the cutting instrument and turned his attention to getting Margaret out of the car.

The searing pain in her head was white-hot. She fought the darkness that was closing around her again. The man pulled at her arms. Her body slumped into the passenger's seat. He had a firm grip now and dragged her out. The moment she was freed from the car, other hands placed her gingerly on a stretcher and rushed her to a waiting ambulance.

A young woman leaned over her and applied a stethoscope

to her chest. She could hear the doors behind her slam shut, feel the ambulance lurch forward and hear the siren shriek.

The pain in Margaret's head was unbearable. Eager to be freed from its intensity, she gave in to the blackness. How long she remained in that state she had no idea.

A stranger's voice cut through the darkness. "Good morning, girl. How are we doing today?"

Light flashed across Margaret's eyelids as she heard the blinds being drawn.

"It's a beautiful, sunny day," the voice continued. "No need to keep you in the dark."

Margaret struggled to open her eyes. She tried her arms. Her legs. Not even her fingers would respond.

A gentle hand smoothed her brow. Her head was lifted as the stranger fussed with the pillow. She could feel the feeding tube tug at her nostril.

"Lord knows you're a sad case, child. Somewhere there's a blessing in all this."

The woman straightened the blanket.

"Lord, bring this dear child through. Give her the strength and courage to face her ordeal."

Face my ordeal? What choice do I have? I certainly can't run away from it, can I?

Now there were other voices in the room: several men and a woman.

Why can't I open my eyes? Who are these people?

Someone lifted her head from the pillow. She felt the bandages being unwrapped and flinched internally as her head was touched. She was rewrapped. Now the endless parade of lights began. Each time her eyelid was held open, she struggled to see beyond the blinding light. She caught a glimpse of movement in the haze, but nothing more. Next, a progression of prodding and poking.

Leave me alone! Will you please just leave me alone and go away!

She wanted to escape from the pain, from the confusion. She searched her memory for some place of refuge.

It was a Sunday afternoon in mid-July. The days had been unusually hot, even for the dog days of summer. The wraparound porch of the old Victorian house offered some solace from the heat. Five-year-old Margaret loved to sit on the porch swing, catching the breezes that blew in from the northwest.

Tom and Jessica were off swimming with friends. Margaret, of course, was too young to go with them.

Her father was asleep on the sofa with a partially read newspaper strewn across his chest and on the floor. An oscillating fan rustled the newspapers at regular intervals.

Mother was in the kitchen, straightening up after a light lunch. She sipped a tall glass of iced tea as she worked.

Friskie, the family's much-loved mutt, whined at the screen door.

"Margaret, let Friskie out on the porch with you," her mother called.

Margaret placed her baby doll on the swing as she climbed down. Friskie left the confines of the house with a leap. He playfully bounced around the girl's feet and then darted off the front porch onto the wide lawn. Margaret laughed as the dog continued his nonsensical acrobatics, chasing after two dancing, white butterflies.

―――――――――CHOICES―――――――――

Margaret climbed back onto the swing. It was not long before Friskie joined her. The two of them lost themselves in each other's company. She never noticed the darkening sky or heard the distant rolls of thunder. It was the chilling flash and deafening crash of a nearby strike that awakened her from her daydream. As if shot from a gun, Margaret bolted into the house with Friskie at her heels.

"Daddy!" she cried.

Her father had been jarred awake and was sitting on the edge of the sofa.

"Daddy, I'm so scared!" Margaret flew into his arms.

"It's all right, Princess. God's just reminding us of who's boss."

Evelyn Beaumont stood in the doorway, looking a bit shaken herself.

"That *was* scary," she said. "It looks as if it did a good job on the Dillons' old apple tree. It's split right down the middle. I sure hope the kids found shelter."

"They'll be fine," her husband assured her.

Another terrifying flash and clap of thunder caused Margaret to tighten her grip on her father. She wished the storm would go away.

"Honey, let's go out on the porch and watch the storm as it moves away," her father said.

Margaret held back.

"Come on. The worst is over. You'll miss something beautiful if you don't come with me."

Timidly, Margaret followed her father out the front door, holding his hand tightly.

A refreshing breeze met them as they stepped onto the porch. Rain was falling, and the cool drops often blew in across the broad span of the porch, splattering their arms and faces. It felt good. Yet, with each flash of the retreating lightning, Margaret winced.

Mr. Beaumont placed two chairs near the door, and they sat down. Soon father and daughter were engaged in watching the awesome show in the sky. With each streak of lightning, they counted the seconds before the thunder boomed. What had only moments before caused great fear now became a game. Margaret laughed, feeling secure on the broad porch.

The agonizing examination was over. Again Margaret had lost all sense of time. Had she fallen back to sleep or been distracted by her memories?

Something was...different. There were shadows and rays of light dancing before her eyes. Although everything around her lay in a thick fog, she was definitely beginning to see. Her eyes had opened on their own. The room was quiet. She relaxed and enjoyed the shafts of light for a while. Having been in darkness for so long, Margaret took great pleasure in this simple experience.

From somewhere in the blur, a figure emerged. It moved to the window and drew the blinds, flooding the room with light. Now it moved toward her, then stopped abruptly.

"Well, look at you, child! Your eyes are open. Thank You, Jesus!"

Margaret's vision began to focus as the woman drew nearer to the head of the bed. She was a well-rounded black woman. Never had Margaret seen such a pleasant face or such a warm smile. The woman was dressed in a crisp nurse's uniform.

"Can you speak, child?"

Margaret tried desperately.

"If you can hear me, blink your eyes."

I can hear you! I can hear you! Oh, eyes, please blink! They've blinked before. Why won't they now?

The nurse patted her patient's hand. "Well, if you do hear me, and just can't respond, let me tell you that you've made quite a bit of progress today. Just relax, and don't worry about anything. You'll be just fine."

The woman continued to work around her, humming softly as she did so. Margaret found comfort in the music and was glad for the company.

The familiar hymn "Rock of Ages" was interrupted by the arrival of the doctors.

"Good morning, Dr. Osborne, Dr. Morris. Look what we have here." The nurse pointed to Margaret's open eyes.

"Well, this is unexpected," one of the doctors said. "Has she responded to you?"

"No, Doctor."

Again the lights shone into her eyes. The poking and prodding began, this time with more than usual intensity. The second doctor jabbed and pushed at her abdomen. He placed his stethoscope on her exposed stomach.

"I want another sonogram," he said. "I don't understand her parents' withholding permission for an abortion. I can't imagine how much money they've spent on lawyers alone."

"You have to admit the pregnancy is progressing far better than any of us expected," Dr. Osborne said.

"Nothing short of a miracle, if you believe in such things. Twenty-five weeks, and everything appears normal."

Twenty-five weeks? That's more than six months! Where have the past three months gone?

"She certainly does make for an unusual case study," Dr. Morris said.

The two doctors left the room.

"Case study, nothing!" The nurse stroked Margaret's

forehead. "You're God's creation, child, and so is this precious little life you're carrying, and don't you ever forget it. And as far as miracles go, I believe in them, and I'm praying for one for you."

Don't waste your time. God's punishing me. He won't take it away that easily.

Margaret stared at the ceiling, her mind whirling with questions. What's wrong with me? Will I ever be able to move or speak again? Is there any hope for me? How can Mom and Dad expect me to have this baby? What kind of mother can I be in this condition? How could God let this happen?

She wished she could cry out in her anguish.

Everything was going to be so simple. Now things couldn't be worse. God, why didn't You just take me?

SIX

MARGARET AWOKE, SENSING SOMEone standing over her. Her eyes spontaneously opened as she regained consciousness, startling her visitor.

Her vision was blurry at first. The scant evening light filtering through the window didn't help much. *Who is it?*

"They said you could open your eyes, but I shouldn't expect any response," the man said. "I guess they're not even sure how much you can hear or see."

John! I never expected to see you again!

"I was in town and thought I should run over to see you before I leave in the morning. I was really shook up when I heard about your accident. I wish I could do something to help you, Margaret."

John just stood there, watching her, for a long time.

"This is difficult for me."

———————CHOICES———————

You ought to try it from my perspective.

He reached down and took her limp hand.

"It's so hard to see you like this. You were so beautiful—so full of life. I wish we could go back to the way things were."

So do I. I'd be walking, talking, laughing and doing all those things I used to take for granted.

"I guess you didn't get the abortion. According to Jenkins, your parents and some pro-life organizations put up quite a battle in the courts."

I'm sorry, John. I tried, but there was this little inconvenience on the way to the clinic.

"Look, Margaret, I can't help but feel some responsibility for your situation. You might say I'm suffering from a guilty conscience. As you know, I'm not in a position to get directly involved with the child. My marriage is too important to me. If my father-in-law ever found out about this, I'd be out on my ear.

"Anyway, if the baby survives, I'll make some arrangement to ensure its financial security."

I guess I'm supposed to be grateful, but it really doesn't impress me, John. Do you think you can free yourself from guilt by opening your wallet? Will that allow you to walk away from here and not give me another thought? While I spend the rest of my life lying here unable even to communicate?

"I enjoyed the times we had together, Margaret. I only wish there could be more such times."

And I wish I had never met you, John T. Farnham. If I hadn't, I might not be here. I certainly wouldn't be pregnant.

John let go of her hand. "I should be going," he said.

He leaned over and kissed Margaret on the cheek.

"I hope someday I'll hear the good news of your recovery. Good luck."

Yeah, sure. Go on—get out of here. And don't come back.

John walked toward the door. In her mind, Margaret picked up the vase of flowers from the nightstand and hurled them after him, splattering water and flowers everywhere.

The next day Margaret awoke to find her mother at her bedside. Evelyn had been at her daughter's side often. Margaret could remember hearing her voice from time to time. All that was hazy, but now she was fully conscious. Her mother's voice was comforting at first. But then Margaret realized her mother was reading from the Bible. A coldness swept over her; she resented the words that had once meant so much to her.

Margaret was twelve. She had looked forward to summer camp ever since the year before. This particular year promised to be the best yet—she would be in the oldest group. The week in the woods was all she had expected. Catching up with old friends, making new ones...she was ready for fun—often at the expense of others. Margaret found it amusing to pull practical jokes on her fellow campers without their finding her out.

It was not so fun for the victims. The food coloring in the toilets may have been funny, but the jelly in Diedra's sneaker and the melted chocolate bar in Ginny's sleeping bag were not. Not even Carolyn, the counselor, was safe from the prankster. When she turned on the water in the sink, she was squirted in the face: Transparent tape placed strategically around the faucet was the culprit.

"Fun is fun, but these practical jokes are going too far," Carolyn said one evening during devotions. Then she prayed,

CHOICES

"Lord, we ask You to convict whoever is doing these things. We ask You to bring her to repentance."

Friday night was always the spiritual highlight of the week. The girls sang songs and shared personal testimonies around the crackling campfire. The camp director ended with an emotional talk, as he had every year Margaret had been attending. For some strange reason she didn't understand, she listened. His words about Jesus, about the pain He suffered on her behalf, touched her deeply.

"There may be some of you here this evening who want to respond to Jesus for what He's done for you," the director said. "We're going to give you that opportunity right now. I'm going to ask all of you to remain in the circle and pray silently for a few minutes. Those who desire to draw closer to the Lord may go over to the pine grove where the counselors will be available to talk and pray with you. The rest of you may return quietly to your cabins."

Margaret looked toward the pine grove. She wanted to go. She felt warmed in a way she couldn't explain. The drawing grew stronger. She looked around. Except for three or four others, everyone else had left. She mustered up her courage and headed toward the pine grove.

"Margaret, may I help you?"

She turned to see Carolyn. She knew what she must do. Jesus would want her to. Tears streamed down her face as she said, "I'm the practical joker. Can you forgive me?"

Carolyn smiled and hugged her. "Of course I can, and I do. And so does God."

They talked a little longer, and then Carolyn led Margaret in a prayer. It was as though heaven broke open and God Himself stood next to her. When the prayer ended, she didn't want to move. She was afraid He would leave. When at last she returned to the cabin, she asked the other girls to forgive her.

The experience remained with Margaret throughout her teenage years. She took a leading role in her church youth group and regularly read her Bible. She even toyed with the idea of following her brother into the mission field.

But that was long ago. So much had happened since then. College marked the beginning of her growing distance from the Lord. Then there was her successful climb up the business ladder. She came to see her accomplishments as exactly that—hers. God was crowded out and eventually became a long-ago memory. Now He was her adversary, punishing her for her sins—at least that's how she saw it. The love she had once felt for Him was now anger toward the one she perceived as her judge.

"...though I walk in the midst of trouble," her mother read, "Thou wilt revive me. Thou wilt stretch forth Thy hand against the wrath of my enemies. And Thy right hand will save me....Oh, Margaret, you're awake."

Yes, Mama, I'm awake.

Evelyn put the Bible aside and drew her chair closer. She stroked her daughter's brow tenderly.

"The doctors don't know for sure just how much you understand, but they think there's a good chance you're understanding something when your eyes are open. I hope it's true."

Oh, Mama, I do understand! I wish I could communicate with you somehow.

"I've rented a room in the city, dear. It was much too hard for your father and me to travel back and forth every day. We were spending over four hours a day in the car. Then when we got home, your father had to take care of the business. We decided it would be much easier on both of us if I stayed in the city during the week, and he came on Saturday to visit you, and then we'd both go home for the rest of the weekend. At least that's the plan until the baby's born. Depending on how things go, we may move you to a nursing home closer to home."

Evelyn Beaumont sat quietly for a time as though waiting for a response. When none came, she continued speaking.

"You look so awake today. I just wish I knew if you were understanding any of this. There are a few things I want to explain to you."

Go ahead, Mama. I'd appreciate some explanations.

"First of all, I want you to know it wasn't easy for your father and me to make the decision about the baby. If you're at all aware of what's going on, you probably think us harsh."

Yes, at least that!

"We *do* love you very much and would like nothing more than to make things as easy as possible for you. Our first reaction was to permit anything that might help save your life. But we just couldn't allow an innocent child to be put to death. We've always taken a stand against abortion. I guess this has been our test, to see if we really meant what we've said—and what a test it's been!"

Evelyn stopped speaking long enough to wipe her eyes.

"We know you had planned on having an abortion, and there's been a lot of pressure on us from some of your doctors, but we won't play God. If the child survives, we'll take responsibility for it. Your father and I aren't so young anymore, but with God's help, we'll make it."

Evelyn was silent again. She rubbed Margaret's limp arm.

"We're trusting the Lord for both of you. Whatever happens will be God's sovereign decision, and we'll accept it as His will. Still, as I said before, we're trusting that you'll both come through this.

"I want you to know, Margaret, that we've forgiven you

for whatever you've done. We'll probably never know all that's gone on in your life, but that's all past now. We're beyond the disappointment and hurt and are determined to glean whatever good we can from this."

Margaret's mother was crying now. She grasped her daughter's hand and kissed it.

"Oh, Margaret, I love you so much. Please, make it!"

Margaret wanted desperately to respond to her mother. Even though she knew it was no use, she tried to move her hand. Nothing. She submitted once again to immobility.

Mother, please don't cry! I'm sorry you had to find out—especially this way. I've hurt you so. I tried so hard to keep the bad things from you. I told you only the things I knew you'd want to hear. I'm just sorry you have to suffer too.

Maybe Jessica wasn't wrong after all. If I'd listened to her and settled down, you wouldn't be crying right now. We'd probably be drinking coffee and watching your grandkids.

Margaret could hear the nurse coming down the corridor toward her room. Her humming always preceded her.

"Good morning, Evelyn," she said as she entered. "I see our girl is wide awake this morning."

"It seems that way, Althea."

Margaret could hear the sound of the blood pressure cuff tightening around her arm.

"So how's your living arrangement working out? You've been there several weeks now, haven't you?" Althea Simpson asked.

"Yes, three. It seems to be working out fine. So far all the boarders seem nice enough. I like the convenience. I can catch the bus at the corner and be here in five minutes."

"As I've said before, if I can do anything for you, just let me know." Mrs. Simpson folded the cuff and jotted down

Margaret's blood pressure on the chart. "I bet you get pretty lonely at night. Maybe we can get together some evening after work and do something."

"That would be nice," Evelyn said. "I do get bored sitting around every evening, watching television shows somebody else picks out."

I know it's hard for you here, Mama. You never did like city life. You always said you'd rather be taken off to jail than live in the city. I know it's a sacrifice for you. I only wish I could tell you how much it means to me.

Completing her examination, the nurse turned Margaret on her side and propped pillows behind her.

"I see you brought a Bible," Mrs. Simpson said.

"Yes, I thought I'd read to Margaret. I don't know if she'll get anything out of it, but it does help me."

"I sure wish I knew what was going on in your daughter's head," Mrs. Simpson said. "I could pray for her proper then. Whatever she's going through, only the Lord can help her with it. If she's locked up in there and can think at all, He's the only one she can talk to."

"There are so many praying for her and the baby," Evelyn said. "We need all the prayer we can get. I won't give up hope."

Spare me the religious talk. When I was younger, I believed God really loved me. Now I don't even want to think about Him. What kind of a loving God would do this to me?

Evelyn Beaumont visited her daughter almost every day. At precisely noon every Saturday, Paul Beaumont arrived. He spent a few hours with Margaret and then took his wife home.

Sunday was an empty day. Usually no one came to visit—

only now and then did Annie or Mr. Jenkins drop in. They never had much to say. Saturday and Sunday were Mrs. Simpson's days off. The other nurses were nice enough—like Mrs. Malecki, the weekend night nurse—but none of them had the same knack Mrs. Simpson had or took as much time with Margaret.

By Monday morning, Margaret eagerly listened for Mrs. Simpson's humming. In spite of herself, she was growing attached to this woman. While she was often annoyed by the nurse's spiritual songs or her prayers, Margaret couldn't deny the loving, tender and competent care that came from this woman's hands.

Late Monday morning her parents would enter the room together. Her father would kiss Margaret and spend a few minutes at her bedside before returning home to begin the work week. Her mother would settle in for another week at Margaret's side.

One afternoon Evelyn gathered up her belongings earlier than usual.

Mrs. Simpson poked her head in the doorway. "Are you ready to go?" she asked.

"Just let me say good-bye to Margaret, and I'll be right with you." Evelyn walked back to Margaret's side and took her hand. "I hope you don't mind my leaving early. Althea and I are going to do a little shopping and then go to her house for dinner. She's becoming a good friend."

Oh, Mama, I'm so happy for you. Yes, do go, and have a good time.

Evelyn Beaumont kissed her daughter on the forehead and hurried out of the room.

The following day Margaret awoke to Mrs. Simpson's rendition of "Swing Low, Sweet Chariot" and the usual flood of light. After the morning ritual and the parade of doctors,

―――――――CHOICES―――――――

Evelyn arrived. She was particularly cheerful and pulled the chair up close to the bed.

"I had a wonderful time last night," she said. "We found all kinds of sales—which, as you know, always lifts my spirits. I bought this sweater for eighteen dollars." Evelyn got up, modeled it and sat down again. "I think this shade of green is just right for my eyes, don't you?"

Yes, it's perfect, Mama.

"After shopping, we went back to her house. She lives in a neighborhood of stately old houses. The properties aren't very large, but there are lots of trees.

"Her husband and two sons are so nice. Did you know her sons were both in college?"

No, Mama, I didn't.

"One's in pre-law, and the other's going to be a history teacher. Her husband is the manager of a large supermarket. We've certainly found a lot in common. After dinner, I went to the mid-week prayer meeting at their church. Margaret, they've got the whole church praying for you."

Wonderful! All I need is to have my shame flaunted before a bunch of strangers! Doesn't anyone think of my feelings?

"I have a surprise for you, Margaret," her mother continued. "I bought several books to read to you. Althea and I both believe you understand even though you don't respond. I thought it would help us both to pass the time if I read a couple of hours each day."

Great idea—as long as it's not the Bible.

The first selection was a current novel Margaret had almost bought just before the accident. She was pleased with her mother's choice and enjoyed the new diversion. It soon became the highlight of each day.

SEVEN

One day the monotony abruptly halted. Margaret, drifting in and out of consciousness, was aware of a flurry of doctors in masks hovering over her, then a ride on a stretcher. She felt as though she were falling through the black void of space and would never be able to return.

A hollow voice, calling her name, drew her back from the edge of oblivion.

"Margaret, Margaret," her father called. "You're going to be all right. You're going to make it. Thank the Lord, you're going to make it!"

Where am I? What happened?

Her eyes opened. She was in an unfamiliar room. The green walls were barren. An array of monitoring devices surrounded her. The medicinal odor in the room was almost overpowering.

─────────────── CHOICES ───────────────

Her mother took her hand tenderly. "Oh, my dear, you have a daughter. She's the sweetest little thing. She was a low birth-weight baby—only four pounds, three ounces—but she's going to make it. We thought we had lost you both, but the crisis seems to be over now.

"The baby arrived four days ago. We took the liberty of naming her. We tried to think of a name you'd like. As a child, you always wanted to have your name changed to Heather. So we're calling her Heather Lynn. I hope you approve." Mrs. Beaumont wiped a tear away with her free hand.

I'm a mother? I don't want to be a mother! What good can I ever be to the child? This is crazy! I can't even move. What...what does she look like? Can I see her? No...no, I don't want to ever see her! I just want to go back into the darkness!

Her father was crying. "Margaret, I hope you understand. How I wish we could communicate, Princess."

Daddy, hold me!

As if hearing her plea, he reached around her shoulders and pulled her to him. She pictured herself on the old porch again. It was as though the lightning had struck, and now the storm was subsiding.

Paul Beaumont lowered his daughter back to the pillow. "We're on the other side of the crisis now, and we'll get through the rest."

Two days later Margaret was back in her old room. To her relief, the familiar schedule resumed. She had missed Mrs. Simpson and was grateful to see her friendly face again.

The blinds opened, allowing the light of day to flood the room.

"Good morning, Margaret," Mrs. Simpson said. "I sure missed you. Thank the good Lord you're back. You put a

─────────── CHOICES ───────────

little scare into me when you started hemorrhaging. But you've come out all right. And that little baby of yours, she's just a little doll. The hit of the nursery, I understand!"

Mrs. Simpson went about her work quietly. She stepped aside when the doctor entered to check his patient. Margaret didn't care much for his bedside manner. He treated her more like an object than a living person.

I'm still a human being here, Doc. Just because I can't yell doesn't mean it doesn't hurt. Take it easy!

The doctor left.

Good riddance!

"You're certainly blessed," said Mrs. Simpson. "You've got such wonderful parents."

She had no sooner finished Margaret's bath when Evelyn came in.

"How's she doing today?" she asked.

"Fine. The doctor seemed to think her progress is good."

"Did he say if they're expecting any improvement now that the pregnancy's over?"

"No, he didn't. You ought to talk to him directly about that."

"Wouldn't it be wonderful if she'd just come out of it?"

"It certainly would. But don't get your hopes up too high. More than likely, you're in for the long haul."

Evelyn sat next to the bed and took the Bible from the drawer.

Oh, Mother, must you?

As her mother read, Margaret tried to busy her mind with her own thoughts, wanting to close out the reading. She managed to ignore it until the very end of the passage.

"He will call upon Me, and I will answer him; I will be with him in trouble; I will rescue him, and honor him. With a long life I will satisfy him, and let him behold My

63

salvation," Evelyn read. "Margaret, I do hope you understand. There's nothing so important to me as knowing you've made your peace with God."

Peace with God? He's the one who put me here. I certainly haven't seen Him coming to rescue me. And how "satisfying" will a long life be if I have to spend it flat on my back? How do you expect me to have peace with God?

The words of the psalm just wouldn't go away, though. They echoed in Margaret's mind. Other words were forming in her mind too—as if printed on an invisible screen. *"But you haven't called on Me for a long time."*

Margaret dismissed the words as the work of her imagination. She turned her attention back to her mother, who was getting up to leave.

So soon? You've only been here a few minutes.

"Margaret, dear, I'll be back shortly. The pediatrician says I should spend time with the baby. It's important for her to be held and loved as much as possible. Of course, I'm more than willing to do it."

Stay with me, Mama. The baby has the nurses. I need you here.

Her mother left.

Great. It's bad enough I have to lie here day after day, totally dependent for everything. Now I have competition for the little attention I do get. The baby's already interfering in my life.

Margaret stared at the ceiling, feeling abandoned. More of the strange words intruded. *"That's a little selfish, isn't it?"*

What is this? I'm not going crazy and hearing voices, am I?

It was a while before Evelyn came back.

"You'll be happy to know that Heather Lynn is doing very well. We can't take her home just yet, though. She has to gain weight first. When we do take her home, we'll be sure to bring her in so you can see her. I wish I could bring her now, but they won't allow her out of the maternity ward until she's released."

I don't ever want to see her! Give her up for adoption. I never wanted her to begin with!

Anger and frustration mounted within her. She wanted to scream. Her chest felt as though it would burst. She thought she was suffocating. She fought to catch her breath.

Margaret could hear her mother calling. "Althea! Something's wrong!"

Her mother's voice drifted away, and Margaret again found relief in the familiar darkness. All sense of time evaded her. Her head was filled with a montage of nonsensical stimuli—lights, sounds, strange physical sensations.

At last some of the sounds took the form of voices.

"Well, she does look better than the last time I saw her," a familiar voice said. "She still had all those tubes going every which way then, and her head was all wrapped up."

It was Jessica. She was the last person on earth Margaret wanted around! Maybe if her eyes didn't open, her sister would go away. Her efforts to control her eyes weren't always successful, but she would try to keep them closed this time. It seemed to be working.

"So," Jessica continued, "do you have any clue yet who the father is?"

"No," Evelyn said. "I'm afraid that'll remain a mystery until Margaret is somehow able to communicate with us."

Mrs. Beaumont rubbed Margaret's hand absently.

"Are you so sure she knows?" Jessica asked.

"Jessica, I don't appreciate that at all!" her mother said.

Neither do I!

"Well, who knows what Margaret's been up to?" Jessica

said. "Obviously, she didn't share much of her life with any of us. None of us even suspected she was pregnant, much less planning an abortion. I sure hope word about *that* doesn't get out. Hugh's always taken a pro-life stand. You can bet someone would pick up on it and use it against him. His political opponents are always trying to find skeletons in the closet."

Always looking out for yourself, aren't you, Jessica?

"And I certainly hope there's nothing else we're going to find out about Margaret," she added. "It makes me nervous."

"I don't think you have to worry about that," her mother assured her. "It's all water under the bridge at this point. What we need now is your support, not your criticism."

"Oh, Mother, there you go sweeping everything under the rug again. When are you going to admit that your little Margaret isn't the angel you'd like to think? She never could do any wrong in your eyes."

"That's quite enough, Jessica," Evelyn said.

"No, it's not 'quite enough'! All my life I tried to do things the right way and make you proud of me, but it was never 'quite enough.' But little Margaret got away with murder."

"That's simply not true!"

"It *is* true, Mother! I know. I know all the times I was punished for what she did."

Margaret could hear Hugh's voice now. "Honey, maybe we should go downstairs and get a cup of coffee."

"Yes, maybe we should. This place gives me the creeps. Is she still breathing?" Jessica said.

"Yes, she's still breathing," her mother said icily.

"We'll meet you in the coffee shop when you're ready to go, Mom," Hugh said.

As Jessica and Hugh left the room, Margaret reflected on

her sister's words. Maybe Jessica had cause for her resentments. One incident came to mind.

The smell of a fresh-baked chocolate cake hung in the air as Margaret entered the house after school. The cake, so warm and fresh, was irresistible. She could not pass it by without a sample. The floor creaked upstairs. Her mother was up there; the coast was clear. She quickly ran her finger along the side of the cake, collecting as much of the gooey, chocolate icing as she could. Then she licked her fingers clean.

"Mmmmmmm."

Margaret could see Jessica coming up the walk. She hurried upstairs to take her school bag to her room. Her mother met her on the landing.

"Well, hello, Margaret. Did you have a good day?" her mother asked.

"Yes, Mommy."

Margaret gave her mother a kiss and continued on to her room. Moments later she heard a shriek from the kitchen. She tiptoed halfway down the stairs and listened to the ensuing conversation.

"Look at this cake!" her mother said. "What do you think you're doing, Jessica? It was for the church supper tonight. I certainly can't take it now."

"Mommy, I didn't do it!"

"Don't lie to me. I see the evidence right there in your hands. If you didn't do it, why are you holding that knife with chocolate all over it?"

"Honest, it was messed up when I came in. I just picked up the knife to smooth it out for you. I was trying to help."

CHOICES

"Don't you lie to me. If you didn't do it, who did?"

"Where's Margaret? Ask her."

Margaret could hear her mother coming into the downstairs hallway. She scrambled back up the stairs and into her room.

"Margaret," her mother called. "Would you come down here for a minute?"

"Coming, Mommy."

She counted to twenty, took a deep breath and went down to the kitchen to face her accuser.

"Margaret, do you know how the icing on this cake got messed up?" her mother asked.

Margaret went to the kitchen table and studied the cake for a moment before answering.

"No. Did you make it for something special?"

"Yes, it was supposed to be for the church supper. Obviously, I can't take it in this condition. You really don't know anything about it?"

"No."

"You're a liar, Margaret!" Jessica cried. "You came home before me and put your greedy little fingers in it. I came home and tried to fix it so Mama wouldn't be upset. Now I'm getting blamed for it. Come on, Margaret, tell the truth."

"I *am* telling the truth."

"She's not, Mommy!"

"That's enough, Jessica," her mother said. "Go to your room. I'll let your father deal with you when he gets home. Just because you're thirteen now doesn't mean you're too old for a spanking."

"I didn't do it! I didn't!"

"Go to your room!" Her mother pointed toward the stairway.

Jessica threw Margaret a cutting look and stormed out of the kitchen.

68

─────────── CHOICES ───────────

That night Margaret sat in her room and listened as her father administered the discipline. She felt bad for Jessica but was glad it was not her bottom being spanked.

I guess there is some truth in what Jessica said, Margaret thought. She did get blamed for a lot of things I did. Is that why she hates me so?

Margaret's eyes opened as she felt her mother take her hand again.

"Oh, you're awake. You just missed Jessica and Hugh. They've been so concerned about you."

Sure, Mom. They love me to death.

"I'm so glad you're with us again, dear. You had another close call. You've got to keep from getting so upset. I can't imagine what's going on in your mind, but you've just got to relax and get well." Evelyn patted her daughter's hand.

I'd rather die!

"You'll be well again. I just know it. Someday you'll just snap right out of it."

Margaret could hear Mrs. Simpson humming her way into the room.

"Margaret's awake," Evelyn said.

The nurse went over to the bed and looked into Margaret's face.

"So she is. That's good. Margaret, we're glad to have you with us again. You've been slipping in and out over the past two weeks."

Two more weeks have passed?

The nurse fluffed the pillows. "So I hear the baby's going home in a few days."

"We hope so," Evelyn said. "She's been doing very

─────────────── CHOICES ───────────────

well—putting on weight. We'll probably be able to take her home early next week. That'll give me a chance to get things in order this weekend."

"Having the baby home is going to make things harder on you, isn't it?"

"I really am torn, Althea. I won't be able to see Margaret except for weekends. It's been a difficult decision to place my granddaughter's welfare above my own daughter's. I wish there were another solution. But after weighing every possibility, this seems to be the best thing."

Althea placed a reassuring hand on Evelyn's shoulder. "Don't worry. You just take care of that little one. She's had a rough beginning, and she's going to need stable family relationships—even if your circumstances *are* a bit unusual. I'll keep an eye on Margaret. I can stay in touch with you by phone during the week and let you know if there are any changes."

"I'd certainly appreciate that. We hope to transfer her to a nursing home as soon as the doctors say she's stable enough to go."

"That would be great. But just don't you worry about her in the meantime. I can even stay a few minutes after work each day and pick up the reading if you like."

Evelyn got up and hugged the nurse. "What would I ever do without you, Althea?"

"What are friends for if they're not there to help one another?"

It was Tuesday. Mrs. Simpson, the doctors and the physical therapist had all been right on time. Evelyn Beaumont was not, but Margaret hadn't expected her to be. Both Evelyn and Paul had been in the evening before and told her that today the baby would go home.

Margaret had slept fitfully during the night and continued to be uneasy about the baby's release from the hospital. She knew this would mean a change in her mother's routine—Margaret would be seeing very little of her mother from this day on. Also, her parents had promised to bring the baby in to see her—something she dreaded.

It was early afternoon before the Beaumonts showed up. Tired from the restless night, Margaret had dozed off while sitting in the lounge chair. Her father's voice awakened her.

"Margaret, can you open your eyes? We have a surprise for you."

Her eyes opened automatically as she woke up with a start.

"Meet Heather Lynn," her mother said.

Margaret's first inclination was to try to close her eyes again and retreat into the darkness. But her fear was overcome by an intense curiosity. She focused on the tiny baby.

"She's so beautiful—just like her mother," Paul Beaumont said.

Margaret stared at the child. Emotions tumbled inside of her.

She *is* beautiful!

Evelyn loosened the blanket so Margaret could see the baby's tiny pink arms and legs.

She's perfect. I guess I've had a hard time believing she could be normal after all we've been through. O God, thank You that she's all right.

Margaret was taken aback as she realized she had just said a sincere prayer. She felt her emotions rising to the surface and tried to control them. She was relieved to see that the child was normal.

Please—you can take her away now. I've seen enough.

———————— CHOICES ————————

Evelyn was holding Heather Lynn directly in front of Margaret. She couldn't keep from looking at her. Just then Heather Lynn's lips puckered, then broadened into what looked for all the world like a smile.

Margaret wanted to laugh out loud. To her surprise, an almost tangible sense of joy surged through her still body. Love seemed to envelop her and spread out to the baby. How she wanted to reach out and touch the little hands and face!

As if sensing her daughter's desire, Evelyn drew close, took Margaret's hand and touched it to Heather Lynn's silky hair and smooth cheeks.

"She is truly a gift from God," Evelyn said.

"Let Margaret hold her," Paul said.

Me? Hold her? I can't!

Evelyn rewrapped the baby carefully. She then placed the little bundle between Margaret's arm and body. Heather Lynn wriggled and squirmed, making baby noises.

I love you so much, my precious little daughter!

And to think, if I had had my way, you wouldn't be here. You are so beautiful! How could I ever have thought about— I can't even say it!

Every cell in her body ached as she wept in silence. The shame and grief she felt were almost too much to bear.

Heather Lynn, how do I ever make up for what I intended to do to you? All I can do is ask you to forgive me. Forgive me, precious little one. You're the best thing that has ever happened to me!

That night Margaret lay in bed, staring at the ceiling. She tried to recall the events of the day in every detail—every feeling, every noise, every movement the baby had made. Joy filled her. But other thoughts pushed the joy aside.

I was actually going to destroy my own baby. How could I—? But maybe God allowed the accident to protect her. O God....

In her mind she knelt beside the bed, her head in her hands.

Lord, it's been so long since I've come to You. I'm not even sure You want to hear me. I've been mad at You and didn't want to have anything to do with You. But please listen.

I've gone my own way and done everything wrong. I got myself into a big mess and tried to get out of it by doing something even worse. But You stopped me from destroying my baby—such a precious little life. God, forgive me! Forgive me! Even if I never get well, I can only thank You for stopping me.

The same peace Margaret had known so long ago returned, stronger than ever before. She knew God had heard her and was answering. The inaudible voice was speaking to her again. *"Take My yoke upon you, and learn from Me, and you shall have rest for your soul."*

Oh, God, I want to! I want to so much. I'll try! From now on I'll try to go Your way! I will!

EIGHT

Now that Evelyn had taken Heather Lynn home, Margaret's days became long and lonely. Mrs. Simpson did everything she could to help Margaret, but her time was limited—she had other patients to care for. The nurse did manage to spend a few minutes after work each day, continuing the reading program.

Yet despite her boredom, Margaret's attitude had changed. Her bitterness and self-pity dissolving, she had even begun to pray. Her times of prayer were awkward at first but grew in richness with each encounter.

Margaret did have Saturdays to look forward to. That was when her mother and father visited. Without fail, the Beaumonts were at her side by 10:00 and stayed until late afternoon.

Always cheerful, Evelyn brought family news of the week's

activities. Naturally, Margaret was captivated most by the detailed reports of Heather Lynn's progress.

While his wife talked, Paul Beaumont sat and read the newspaper from cover to cover. He often interrupted with something of interest. Margaret was grateful for the diversion.

One Saturday morning her father put his newspaper aside and moved near the bed.

"Have you told her yet?" he asked his wife.

Margaret looked on, waiting for what seemed to be special news from her parents. Evelyn shook her head no. Paul took his daughter's hand tenderly.

"Princess, your little girl has been given quite a large gift. We don't have any idea who the benefactor is, though we assume it must be the baby's father. Anyway, a lawyer came to see us Thursday evening and told us that a $50,000 trust fund has been set up for Heather Lynn. That plus the insurance settlement puts you both in a pretty good place financially."

He did it, Margaret thought. John kept his word.

"I sure wish you could tell us who the father is. I'd really like to talk with him," Paul said.

Sorry, Daddy. Even if I could speak, I wouldn't tell you. It's best to just let it be.

Paul was studying his daughter's face more intently than usual.

"Evelyn," he said. "I do believe I just saw a spark of understanding in Margaret's eyes."

"I know. It's just so frustrating not knowing how much she comprehends," her mother said. "I can't imagine how bored she must be just lying here all day."

"Princess," Paul said, "how would you like to have the television turned on? It would help you pass the time."

I'd love it! Anything to keep my mind busy.

"I'm going to go downstairs and have it switched on. I'm sure Mrs. Simpson and the other nurses wouldn't mind turning it on and off."

As he left the room, Margaret thought back to another time in her childhood—another time when her father had rescued her from boredom.

Ten-year-old Margaret had gone to the hospital early in the morning to have her tonsils taken out. Her mother had stayed by her side most of the day, but her father had to work. It was evening before he arrived at the hospital to take them home.

How comforted she felt as he picked her up and carried her out the door!

"Oh, my little princess, I wish I could have been with you."

Margaret tried to speak but couldn't. Her throat was too sore.

"Don't try to speak, honey. You have many years to make up for this short period of silence."

Arriving home, Paul carried his daughter into the house. Up the intricately carved staircase they made their way, through the door to her bedroom. She felt secure back in the spacious room. The sight of the flowery wallpaper and the crisp white curtains in the dormer window brought her untold delight. Here she was at home with all her friends as they peered down from the shelves on either side of the window. Her dolls, teddy bears and other stuffed animals seemed relieved to have their mistress home.

She snuggled down in the old four-poster bed. The cool sheets felt good against her skin. Soon she fell asleep, and when she awoke, her father was by her side.

"How are you doing, Princess?"

Margaret smiled and nodded her head as if to say, "Just fine, Daddy."

"I brought you some surprises to keep you busy while you're recuperating."

He pointed to a pile of brightly wrapped packages on the nightstand. Margaret reached for them excitedly.

"Hold on, young lady! There are some rules you must follow. You may open only one right now. You may not open another until you're done with the first. From then on you may have another only when you've exhausted the one before it."

Margaret was eager to plow into the gaily decorated gifts, but she obeyed her father. She picked one out and opened it. It was a pad of paper and some markers.

She immediately drew a picture of a smiling girl and, in brightly colored letters, wrote, "THANK YOU, DADDY."

"You certainly are welcome, sweetheart. You just hurry up and get well."

In the days that followed she was grateful for her father's instructions to ration the gifts. Her time in bed became pleasant, knowing there was always another surprise to be opened.

An activity book came next, followed by a sticker book, a bag of comic books and many other childish delights. In later years she realized they were just items her father had around the pharmacy. But at the time they were worth a million dollars. Best of all was the fact that her father had taken the time to gather them together and wrap them.

In her present condition Margaret couldn't open any presents. But here was her father, again seeking a way to

———————— CHOICES ————————

help her through a difficult time.

The next day the television was turned on. Whenever she wasn't being examined, having therapy or sitting in the hall in the lounge chair, Margaret was propped up in the hospital bed watching television—a very pleasant distraction from her monotonous existence.

On one occasion Mrs. Simpson turned on the set and left the room. The program was a talk show, one that always promised a lively, heated discussion.

"Are you telling us, Senator, that there are members of Congress who are actively considering such a bill?" the host was asking.

"Yes, I am. I don't believe passage of such a bill is imminent, but it is on the horizon. I don't think we can afford to ignore the possibility. With the sharp increase in numbers of senior citizens, and a decrease in the supporting work force, there simply won't be enough of a tax base to meet the need—that's not even taking into account the burden the AIDS epidemic has placed on our health care system. Medical treatment is already at a premium in many areas of our country, and the cost is becoming prohibitive for a growing portion of our society. In years to come we will be forced to pick and choose who is to get that help."

"But, Senator," a woman on the panel interrupted, "you're not just suggesting a system for choosing who will get medical help, nor are you simply turning off life-support systems—you're proposing a law which will provide for the systematic murder of our elderly and infirm by lethal injection."

"We prefer to use the word 'release.' "

"Yes, that is a more palatable term. But what I'd like to know is who would have the authority to decide whether someone was to be 'released,' as you put it."

"Mrs. Nielson, I realize your organization and I are at

opposite ends of the scale on this subject, and I'm sure you consider me heartless in the matter, but I really do want to stress the importance of weighing each and every individual case. The criterion must be whether or not an individual is experiencing, or has the potential to experience, a meaningful life. There would be a group designated to make this determination, a group made up of professionals such as doctors, lawyers, physical therapists, social workers and others. Still, the final decision must remain with the family."

"Let's take, for instance, an individual who has been paralyzed in an accident," the host said. "How long would it be before a committee might determine that his or her quality of life had diminished enough to permit termination?"

Margaret listened with horror. They were talking about *her!*

"I've heard my colleagues suggest a time period anywhere from three months to a year," the senator answered. "Again, I feel each case must be weighed on its own merits. In some cases it will be almost immediately evident that a significant loss of function has occurred which would make release expedient for all involved. In other cases the progression of the debilitation may not be as visible, and a much longer period of time may be required. We need the professionals to tell us what the possibilities are for future recovery. I can't emphasize enough that every aspect must be considered before a decision is made."

The host turned his attention to the third member of the panel. "Mr. Stanley, you represent the health insurance companies. What benefits, if any, would such legislation have for your industry?"

"I would have to say that the benefits would not be so much for the insurer as they would be for the insured. It all goes right back to dollars and cents. It's no secret that medical costs are sky-high, taking insurance prices with them. If health insurance isn't going to skyrocket beyond the reach of all but the most wealthy, we need to become more cost efficient. I believe the health insurance industry would eagerly welcome a proposal that would allow them to cut off benefits should an individual become eligible for release. I imagine public assistance programs would quickly follow suit and cancel benefits to those in this category. I can foresee that it would save hundreds of millions of dollars in health care costs and in social security."

Mrs. Nielson could no longer keep quiet. "In other words, if you want your loved one to live, you had better have the money for it. I strongly support the concept of personal responsibility, but in this case it seems more like a ploy to force people to kill off their loved ones. I can't imagine what that would mean for this nation. I fear the majority of our citizens won't even flinch at such a proposal, Senator. Our national conscience has already become so calloused that an atrocity such as this might not even touch it. There's a whole generation of young adults out there who have been brought up believing there's nothing wrong with killing babies for convenience' sake. I don't think it will be too difficult for them to accept the mass elimination of the elderly for the same reason."

"Mrs. Nielson," the senator said, "I respect your concern for the individual, and, as I said before, we cannot overlook the value of each person. But we must also weigh the burden placed on society by these...."

Margaret was so engrossed with the program she didn't hear the orderlies entering the room. The television was turned off, and she was moved onto a stretcher.

Couldn't you have waited a few more minutes? I suppose you're taking me for more prodding and poking. I could no more resist being taken to the slaughter than

―――――――――― CHOICES ――――――――――

I can keep from going with you right now.

Margaret was being wheeled through the corridor to the elevator. She had no idea of her destination.

I have nothing to fear. Mom and Dad have strong beliefs with respect to life. They would never allow anything like that to happen to me. I have nothing to worry about—as long as they're around to protect me.

NINE

MARGARET WAS CAREFULLY PLACED on a bed in an unfamiliar room. The orderlies left while a nurse checked her permanent feeding tube and catheter.

"Welcome to third floor east," the woman said.

Am I here to stay? Margaret wondered.

The nurse checked her pulse. Next would be the blood pressure.

I want to go back to Mrs. Simpson's floor. I don't want to be here. Take me back!

"Are you hungry? As soon as I finish taking your blood pressure, I'll get you some lunch."

How about a hamburger and french fries this time?

The nurse rolled up the blood pressure sleeve and jotted her notations on the chart. She left the room briefly and returned with a can of liquid, which she emptied into the bag that hung over Margaret's head.

Margaret stared blankly at the ceiling. I hope Mrs. Simpson doesn't forget about me.

Strange noises came from the bed next to her.

I have a roommate. Hello, my name's Margaret. What's yours?

Her silent question was answered by more garbled sounds.

You're not much of a conversationalist.

"Well, there you are," came a familiar voice from the doorway.

Mrs. Simpson! Thank God—you found me!

"Congratulations! You've gotten yourself promoted from critical care to custodial care. This floor is like a nursing home. I knew you were going to be transferred soon, but I didn't think it was going to be that quick. You'll probably be here until your folks find a nursing home closer to home. Meanwhile, I guess you'll have to put up with me poking my head in from time to time."

Margaret wasn't sure she liked the idea of leaving the hospital—it had become her security. It was hard enough to change floors, much less be moved to an entirely different place.

"Here, I brought your things." Mrs. Simpson went about putting Margaret's few personal items away, humming as she did so. "Now I've got to get back to my own floor. But don't you worry none. I'll be back to do our reading before I go home. You just behave yourself and don't give the nurses any trouble."

Yes, ma'am!

More noises drew Margaret's imagination back to the occupant of the next bed.

I wonder who she is and what's wrong with her. Well, it'll be a new source of entertainment—at least until I get my television reinstated. I can play detective. I'll just lie here, gather bits of information, and put together a personality profile.

She learned the woman's name—Ruth—from a nurse who scolded the woman for not staying still when she took a blood sample. Later a middle-aged woman entered and called the woman "Mom." By late evening, Margaret had Ruth's history down pat. She was an elderly diabetic recovering from a stroke which left her partially paralyzed on her right side. Her speech was also affected. She too was awaiting nursing home placement.

Ruth's slurred speech continued throughout the night, making it difficult for Margaret to sleep. She asked God to help her be quiet. It seemed to Margaret that Ruth's talking stopped almost immediately, but then maybe she just fell asleep and didn't hear the woman carrying on. Whatever happened, Margaret was grateful for the rest.

Another Saturday arrived. Margaret hadn't seen Heather Lynn for several weeks. She hoped her parents would bring her, even though their visit would have to be shorter than usual.

Two nurses had just moved Margaret to a lounge chair and pushed her into the hall when she saw her parents. Yes, they did bring Heather Lynn.

"There's your mama," Margaret heard her mother say.

Heather Lynn was all dressed up in a pretty pink dress and white tights. A pair of handmade booties graced her little feet, which always seemed to be in motion.

How quickly you change, Margaret thought. I wouldn't know you from one time to the next. Oh, how I wish I could hold you and take care of you.

Paul brought a chair from her room and placed it close to the lounge chair. Evelyn sat down and held the baby next to Margaret. Margaret could see a little hand reach out and grip her fingers. She wanted to respond but knew she couldn't.

You are so pretty. Your hair is starting to grow, and it's getting curly. Your eyes get bluer every time I see you. You're going to be a knockout, Heather Lynn.

By now all the nurses were gathering around to see the baby.

I wish I could tell you just how happy I am. Even if I could communicate, there's no way I could say how important you are to me. Your smile and your energy keep me going. I hope someday you'll know the joy you are to me.

In her imagination Margaret was picking up her daughter and snuggling her. She was holding Heather Lynn tightly in her arms as she danced down the corridor. In this realm she was free from the limitations of her paralyzed body and could soar.

The imagery was shattered by a sudden wail.

What's wrong, Heather Lynn?

"I think all the attention might be too much for her," Paul said.

The nurses started to leave.

"I'll take her for a little walk while you talk to Margaret," Evelyn said.

Paul sat down. "Princess, the doctors seem to think you're well enough to leave here soon and go to a nursing home. We've been looking around for one close to home and think we may have found one that fits the bill. It's not the fanciest, but it's homey and only twenty minutes from the house. It would mean we'd be able to visit you more often. We've put your name on the waiting list. As soon as there's an

———————————— CHOICES ————————————

opening, you'll be transferred. It could take a while, but when it happens, there may not be much advance notice."

That sounds great, Daddy. It would be so good to see you and Heather Lynn more often. But it's scary to think about leaving the hospital. I've been here so long. I can hardly remember what lies beyond these walls.

Margaret anticipated moving in a few weeks. But when the weeks turned into months, she all but forgot about a change. Then one morning the waiting came to an end.

"No, just put all her personal belongings in a box," the nurse said to an orderly. "They'll be delivered later."

Everyone spent more time than usual with her this morning and wished her well as they left. Soon two orderlies placed her on a stretcher and pushed her down the corridor to the elevator.

Wait a minute! This is too fast! I haven't had a chance to say good-bye to Mrs. Simpson.

She tried to look around, hoping she would see the dear woman, but her line of vision was quite limited. Mrs. Simpson was nowhere to be seen.

Margaret fought back her anxiety. Yes, she was eager to be close to home. But she was apprehensive about starting over again someplace else—a whole new routine and staff to get used to.

Margaret thought the trip would never end. She tried to close her eyes to escape the sensation of motion sickness, but it didn't help. Finally, the ambulance rolled to a stop.

As the stretcher was lowered to the sidewalk, Margaret strained to catch a glimpse of her new home. The little she saw gave her some comfort. It was reminiscent of her family's Victorian home: a stately old house with broad porches and two modern wings which jutted out on either side. The center portion, although larger, appeared to be about the same age and style as her parents' house. The lawns, carefully manicured and shaded by ancient trees, spread out as far as her eyes could see. It was early spring, and all nature seemed to be bursting forth with fragrance and color, making the property even more appealing.

Margaret took in one last breath of fresh air before being rolled into the building. The interior was as pleasant as the exterior. A sweeping staircase commanded attention in the large entry. The rich woodwork again evoked childhood memories. Margaret liked the place.

A receptionist sat at a desk to one side of the staircase. She greeted them, then picked up the phone and made a call. Moments later a nurse joined them and led them to an elevator. They got out at the second floor. To Margaret's delight they did not go into one of the newer wings but entered a room in the older section.

The room had two beds. The one farthest from the door was occupied. Margaret was placed on the bed near the door and left with her head elevated, making it possible to see her new surroundings.

Yellow walls reflected sunlight that shone through the large bay window opposite her bed. Crisp white curtains framed the window, just as they had in her own room at home. Pictures of landscapes and flowers perched on the walls.

Outside the window stood a strong, gnarled oak which was entertaining two frolicking squirrels in its branches. Margaret became enthralled with this new diversion and was completely oblivious of what was going on in the room.

"Hello, Margaret, dear," she heard her mother say, calling her back to her more immediate surroundings.

Mrs. Beaumont leaned over and kissed her daughter.

"I hope you had a pleasant trip. I also hope you're happy with this place. We were so relieved when a bed opened up in the old section. We thought it would be more homey here than in one of the newer wings."

Oh, Mama, it's just perfect!

"And as soon as you settle in, we'll be able to take you for walks on the grounds. There'll be a lot more freedom here than in the hospital. Best of all, you'll be able to see Heather Lynn more often."

Margaret looked forward to the many small pleasures which would be hers again. So many everyday experiences had been out of reach for so long, she barely had hope of rediscovering them. Just the sensation of a breeze on her face and the warmth of the sun had delighted her beyond measure. She no longer took such simple pleasures for granted.

The next afternoon, Evelyn brought Heather Lynn with her. It had been a month since Margaret had seen her, and the child had changed tremendously. There was great satisfaction knowing she would now see her baby every few days rather than once a month.

Heather Lynn was wide awake and bubbling over with little baby noises. She gave Margaret a big smile which lit up her entire face.

Heather Lynn, thank you for accepting me now. But I just wonder how long it'll be before you see your mother as a freak.

Margaret shuddered at the thought of this happy little girl not wanting to come and see her.

Will you be afraid when you know about me? As a teenager, will you hate me because I'm an invalid you have to visit? Will I ever be able to tell you how much I love you?

A few days later Margaret was surprised by another visitor. "Margaret, how are you doing?" said a familiar voice.

―――――――― CHOICES ――――――――

Mrs. Simpson! What are you doing here?

"I just couldn't stay away. I felt terrible that I didn't get to see you before they transferred you. I got caught up in an emergency and couldn't get down to the third floor until you had already gone. Anyway, I brought you all your things. George and I are visiting your folks. As you know, we've become quite close over the past year, and there's no reason it should stop now. I'll be popping in from time to time when I get down this way."

That's wonderful! I've missed you so much!

Margaret's mother stepped into view.

"George is visiting with your father and babysitting while we ladies are here," she said.

"My, your little one is growing up so fast," Althea said. "She's all over the place. Your mother's going to stay trim keeping up with her."

She pulled a colorfully wrapped package out of her bag. "I brought something for you, honey."

Althea tore off the bright pink bow and paper. Inside was the plumpest, fluffiest, stuffed polar bear Margaret had ever seen.

It's adorable! Thank you.

"You may think it's a funny gift, Margaret, but I just couldn't resist getting it for you. You might like to have it around whenever Heather Lynn is here."

You are so thoughtful, Mrs. Simpson. Thank you.

Althea moved a chair next to Margaret and talked while Evelyn put Margaret's personal belongings away.

"Look what I have," Evelyn said, holding up a book.

Margaret could see the title. It was *The Hobbit*. Althea had been reading it to her when she was transferred.

"We can pick up where Althea left off, right now," she said.

───────────CHOICES───────────

The two women sat side by side, taking turns reading chapters out loud.

Life in the nursing home was a considerable improvement over the hospital schedule. Hospital gowns were replaced with real clothes, and every few weeks a beautician would do her hair. Some physical therapy was continued—at least enough to keep her arms and legs from stiffening.

During the first week her father had brought her a television, which was turned on a few hours each day. There were more visits from family and friends, as well as excursions around the grounds. Added to these activities was the most pleasant addition of all—occasionally going home for a few hours on holidays.

The days, weeks, months and years went by. There was no real change in Margaret's condition over those years. In the meantime, Heather Lynn was growing up.

TEN

NEWLY FALLEN SNOW CRUNCHED UNDERfoot as Margaret was carried from the car to the front porch. It took all three men—her father, her brother and her nephew Elias—to get her home in the snow. Although she weighed very little, balancing all her paraphernalia made moving her a major undertaking. But no one minded. No amount of trouble was too much. They were bringing Margaret home for Christmas.

Margaret caught the heavy scent of balsam in the air as she was brought into the front hallway. Her father strapped her into her wheelchair and pushed her into the living room. Sunlight flooded the room, reflected off the clean, white snow through the broad windows. The Christmas tree, bedecked with shining ornaments and brightly colored lights, stood in the large bay window where all its predecessors had stood

―――――――――― CHOICES ――――――――――

before it. A fire blazed in the fireplace, warding off the morning cold.

Heather Lynn ran down the stairs to greet her mother with a hug and a kiss. "Merry Christmas, Mommy."

Merry Christmas, sweetheart. You look absolutely beautiful. I can't believe how fast you're growing.

Evelyn came through the dining room from the kitchen, followed by Sally and Elizabeth. They each leaned down to give Margaret a kiss.

"Merry Christmas, dear," her mother said. "We were so worried last night when it started to snow. They weren't sure how many inches we were going to get, and we were afraid a large snowfall would make it hard for us to get you over here this morning. I'm so glad you're here."

I'm glad too, Mama.

"As you can see, Jessica and Hugh aren't with us. They're spending the holidays with his family. They said to wish you a merry Christmas."

Oh, sure. Jessica and Hugh haven't spent Christmas with us since the first Christmas I came home after the accident—nine years ago. It's obvious why they don't come—me! Actually, I'm glad they don't come. And I'm not going to let them ruin this special day.

"OK, gang, now that we're all here, let's get these gifts unwrapped," Paul said. "Heather Lynn, you can pass them out as usual."

Heather Lynn jumped to the task of handing out the gayly decorated packages. She was particularly attentive to her mother, often leaving her own gifts to embrace or kiss Margaret. She would then return to opening her presents. She was especially excited as she opened the gifts marked "With love from Mommy." The first was a beautiful, warm coat.

94

CHOICES

Heather Lynn ran over and hugged her mother again.

"I know you didn't pick this out, Mommy, but I know you would have if you could."

Yes, I would have, and I would've bought you so much more.

The second gift given in Margaret's name was always something Evelyn had packed away in the attic. This year it was Margaret's wooden jewelry box. Heather Lynn was thrilled and ran over to express her happiness to her motionless mother.

"I bought something for you, Mommy." She picked from under the tree a small but elegantly wrapped package. "I'll help you open it."

The girl tore open the gift and displayed its contents with pride. "It's perfume. It's the expensive kind. It's called *Sophia*." She unscrewed the top and placed it under her mother's nose.

The scent brought Margaret great pleasure. She couldn't remember the last time she had smelled perfume. Most of the time her nostrils were filled with medicinal odors.

Heather Lynn dabbed a little drop behind her mother's ears.

Thank you, dear. You're so thoughtful—a trait you've learned from your grandparents, no doubt.

All too soon, it seemed, the last of the gifts had been opened.

"Before we start clearing up this mess," Tom said, "let's move Margaret to the bed. She's due for a change of position."

Soon Margaret was lying comfortably on the hospital bed that was kept in the corner of the living room for such visits. From there she could feel a part of the family activities, yet still rest when she wanted to.

She could hear the crumpling of paper, which meant the clean-up was underway. The fire crackled as the paper was thrown into the fireplace. Elias and Elizabeth, now both in college, laughed at Heather Lynn's antics, which Margaret couldn't see from her vantage point.

Margaret knew the dinner hour was approaching by the smell of ham emanating from the kitchen. It had been a long time since she had tasted real, honest-to-goodness food. But her memory of how it tasted was sharp. How she longed to join the feast!

Evelyn and Sally were setting the dining room table, judging from the clatter of plates and clink of silverware Margaret heard. They were whispering, but her keen ears picked up the conversation.

"I just can't believe Jessica is so ignorant and stubborn," Sally said. "Not wanting to 'expose her children to Margaret's distasteful circumstances'! Who does she think she is? Where's her heart? I should think she could put herself aside for a few hours for your sake."

"Well, Sally dear, our Jessica has strange ideas. Margaret is a terrible embarrassment to her, and she just doesn't know how to handle it."

"With all her charity work, it would be nice if she had a little more compassion for her own sister—and a little more respect for her mother."

"It's probably better this way. Jessica's presence here would just cause tension for all of us. I love my daughter, but sometimes even I can't...."

The two women had returned to the kitchen and could no longer be overheard.

God forbid that Jessica's life ever be interrupted by some unforeseen tragedy, Margaret thought. She'd never survive it.

She remembered the previous spring, when Jessica had made her annual pilgrimage to her sister's bedside. Margaret was lying on the lounge chair, staring out the window when Jessica came in.

"Hello, Margaret. It's your big sister, Jessica."

Oh...hello, Jessica. Is it that time of year again?

Margaret wished there were some way to escape the situation. She thought she might try to close her eyes and feign falling asleep. On that particular occasion her eyelids would not cooperate, however, and she was forced to bear Jessica's chatter.

"It's good to see you looking so well. I do wish you could speak. I miss talking with you, and there's so much for us to talk about."

I wish I could talk too. I'd tell you to go away. You don't have to come here and pour out your pity on your invalid sister. It's not going to clear your conscience.

"Remember the long talks and good times we used to have?"

Yes, as a matter of fact, I do. Our talks were usually yelling matches at each other.

"Those times are just so precious in my memory—especially now that there's no hope....Well, anyway, I just keep hoping you'll get better soon, and we'll have those times again."

Oh, Jessica, who do you think you're fooling? Certainly not me.

Margaret made another desperate attempt to blot out her sister's presence by closing her eyes. But she couldn't blot her out, and Jessica continued her monologue, boring Margaret with her family's activities and many accomplishments.

Margaret's thoughts returned to the present at the sound of her father's voice.

"How are you doing, Princess?"

As well as can be expected, I guess.

"This has been one of the best Christmases I can remember. Only one thing would make me happier, and that would be for you to be well. But I am so grateful just to have you here with us."

The gray-haired man lightly brushed the corner of his eye. "And, Princess, you have such a beautiful daughter. I'm sure you're just as proud of her as we are. We're doing the best we can with her. It isn't easy for any of us, but Heather Lynn is worth it all. Someday we'll understand. But at least for now, please don't ever be bitter or resent God for what's happened."

"Dinner's ready," Evelyn called.

Margaret's father continued. "It's been a busy day for you. You need to rest. I don't feel much like eating, but I'll do my best to eat my share and make your mother happy. I love you, Princess."

Paul Beaumont kissed his daughter on the forehead and checked her for comfort before taking his place at the dinner table. Margaret's eyes were heavy, and it wasn't long before she dozed.

By the time Margaret awakened, the atmosphere in the old house had changed dramatically. She could hear crying and strange voices coming from the dining room. Something was very wrong.

What's going on? Margaret cried inaudibly.

She lay on the hospital bed for a long time, her heart pounding. She glimpsed a stretcher being rolled out of the dining room, across the living room and out the front door to the porch. Seconds later a siren blasted as the ambulance left. Now her heart raced.

Heather Lynn came to Margaret's side. Crying hysterically,

she climbed up on the chair next to the hospital bed and leaned over her mother, burying her face in Margaret's neck.

"Mommy, it's Grandpa," the little girl sobbed. "They took him away. He's really sick. He'll be OK, won't he?"

Daddy? No, no, not him!

She tried desperately to squeeze her daughter's hand in comfort. She wanted so much to let Heather Lynn know she shared the pain.

Sally approached the bed. Her expression betrayed how shaken she felt.

"Heather Lynn," she said, "I want you to stay here with Elizabeth. Uncle Tom went to the hospital with your grandmother, and I'll be going with Elias to take your mother back to the nursing home. Then we'll go on to the hospital."

"But, Aunt Sally, I want to stay with Mommy!"

Sally gently pulled the girl away from Margaret and held her close to her. "Honey, I know you hurt inside. We all do. I don't want to take your mother back so early, but we have to. We need to think about your grandpa right now."

Elizabeth took her young cousin by the hand. "Come on, Heather Lynn. Your mom needs to go back where she can be cared for. And we need to stay here and help out."

Elizabeth is right, dear.

The child broke away, then ran back to kiss her mother good-bye. She stepped back to let Sally and Elias move Margaret to the wheelchair, then out to the car. Margaret could still see her daughter standing on the porch, watching, as they turned the car around.

Margaret slept fitfully that night. It wasn't until the next afternoon that Tom and Sally came in. Tom turned off the TV and knelt down next to the lounge chair where Margaret was sitting.

"Sally and I just came from the hospital," Tom said. "We knew you'd want to hear about Dad. It doesn't look good, Margaret. The damage to his heart was pretty bad. He's in critical condition."

But he's still alive, Margaret thought.

"We're on our way now to take Heather Lynn and Elizabeth to the hospital. I hope I'll be able to bring you better news soon. Keep praying in the meantime. We'll be back as soon as we can."

"We wish we could stay longer," Sally said, "but we really do need to pick up the girls and get back."

I understand. Thank you for coming.

Sally and Tom kissed Margaret and left.

Two days passed before anyone else came. It was early evening. Margaret had just been put to bed when her mother entered the room with Tom. Evelyn was pale, and her eyes were red from crying.

"Margaret," she said, "I know you've been waiting to hear something about your father. I wanted to come but just couldn't."

Evelyn was choked up and had to stop speaking for a few minutes.

Please, Mama, tell me!

Finally, she said, "Your father died yesterday afternoon."

She was crying. Tom held her, tried to comfort her.

Margaret was crying too, although there was no outward show of her grief. Inwardly, every cell of her body resounded with the silent echoes of her groans.

Oh, Daddy, you can't be gone! We all need you so—

especially Mama. Please, God, no, not Daddy. Not now.

"The funeral will be the day after tomorrow. I hope it's the right thing to do, but I want you there."

Oh, yes, Mama. Please, yes—I must go.

The morning of the funeral found Sally, Tom and Heather Lynn at the nursing home early. Any other time Margaret would have enjoyed the extra attention, but not today. Sally brushed Margaret's hair and gently fitted her frail body into a new dress. She was strapped into the wheelchair and taken to a waiting medi-van.

It had snowed lightly the day before, but the roads were clear. The beauty of the day stood in stark contrast to the sorrow it held.

As Margaret was wheeled up the ramp to the church door, Jessica and Hugh arrived. They barely acknowledged Margaret as they entered the vestibule, solemnly greeting friends and family. Although Jessica pulled her mother aside, their conversation was not missed by any in the entry—least of all Margaret.

"How could they bring Margaret to the funeral?"

"They, Jessica? *I* insisted that Tom and Sally bring her."

"How could *you*, then? It's awful! She isn't even aware of what's going on around her. How could you make a spectacle at your own husband's funeral?"

"I'm sorry if you're embarrassed, Jessica. I'm not. The only person making a spectacle of herself is you! I don't want to hear another word from you."

"Well, I just...."

Evelyn's face was red with anger. "Margaret is as much

————————CHOICES————————

your father's daughter as you are. She has every right to be here, and I suspect she understands far more than you do. She would be very upset if she didn't get to say good-bye to her father. If you have a problem with that, then you can just pack your family up and go home. I don't need any more remarks from you today."

That's telling her, Mama!

Margaret wanted to stand up and cheer.

Heather Lynn placed her small hand on her mother's. Margaret turned her attention to her daughter, who did not leave her side throughout the service.

Many old friends, including the Simpsons, came and greeted Margaret after the funeral. Many seemed very uncomfortable, but she was touched by their efforts.

Just as she was being strapped in the medi-van, her mother climbed in and knelt beside her chair. She took Margaret's hand in hers.

"We'll be OK," she said. "Don't worry about a thing. I know God is still watching over us."

I know He is too. I just wish I could help you.

Margaret couldn't fall asleep. Even though she was tired from the day's events, her thoughts were whirling.

She remembered her father's last words to her. It was as if he knew he was saying good-bye and he wanted her to know he did not resent her. Ever since she first saw Heather Lynn, Margaret had wanted to assure her father and mother she wasn't bitter toward them, either.

Maybe he knows now.

As she lay on her bed, she pondered the day's events. Although her mother had tried to reassure her, Margaret knew she would be lost without the man she had cherished and depended upon for almost fifty years. She would be very lonely.

Lord, You know what Mama's going through. She really needs You. She loves You so much. Please help her. She knows You love her, but please show her too. Keep Your arms around her—and around Heather Lynn too.

That night Margaret fell asleep, just as she had when she was a child and knew her heavenly Father was watching over her.

ELEVEN

VISITORS WERE SPORADIC IN THE WEEKS following the funeral. With fewer diversions Margaret's thoughts often turned to her father. She recalled everything she could about him—his eyes, his hair, his love. The pain of missing him was very deep.

A nurse entered the room.

Daddy, is that you?

No, he's gone, she reminded herself time and time again. And he won't be back.

Even though she was eager to have company, Margaret was more than grateful that Jessica kept her distance.

It was different with Tom and Sally. They always treated her like a normal person. They seemed to understand her feelings and thoughts and would even answer her unspoken questions. And they brought Heather Lynn with

CHOICES

them as often as possible.

But Margaret knew that as missionaries they would leave again. She wished they could stay.

"It's time we had a serious talk," Tom said one February afternoon. "I hate to even bring the subject up, but I have to. As you know, Margaret, we have only five months left of our furlough, then we'll be heading back to New Guinea. At least that's our plan, God willing."

I hope He's not willing. Mama needs you here. So do I.

"I hope to use the remaining time to get Mom into a more secure situation. My greatest concern is the pharmacy. Carl Porter, the pharmacist, will stay on, but I need to find someone reliable to take over as manager when I leave."

I wish I could do it!

"I just want to assure you that, if we don't find someone we can really trust, we'll postpone our return to the mission field until we do."

I'm all for that. Do you think God would mind if I prayed that you don't find anybody? That way you'd have to stay indefinitely. No, I suppose that's too selfish. You have your own lives to live. I can't expect you to give up your hopes and dreams to suit my purposes.

"The mission needs us to get back there when we're expected, so I hope we find someone pretty quick."

Well, Tom, I'll pray for that, even though I'd much rather keep you right here. I know you've got to get back.

It was a bright spring morning. Margaret awoke with a start. For a moment she had lost her orientation. Something had sparked memories of long ago when she was still in the hospital.

———————— CHOICES ————————

A nurse was opening the blinds. "Good morning, ladies. And how's my old friend Margaret this morning?"

The voice was familiar somehow, as was the plump, graying woman who came over and took her hand. "I bet you're surprised."

Mrs. Simpson! What on earth are you doing here?

"I'm a little surprised myself, girl. This all happened so fast. Your brother approached George a month or so ago and asked if he'd be interested in managing the pharmacy. The salary was less than what he received at the supermarket, but we figured the cost of living here would be less than in the city. We've always dreamed of living in the country, so we decided to step out in faith and accept.

"I gave notice at the hospital, and the last time I was here I put in my application. Two days ago they called and said I could have the job if I could start right away. One of their nurses had quit and her replacement only lasted a week. They were desperate, so I came right down. I'll be staying with your mother until we sell our old place and buy a house down here.

"So, my dear, I guess you're stuck with me again, at least until I retire."

Oh, Mrs. Simpson, that's wonderful! I hope you *never* retire!

"Girl, is that a smile I see on your face?" The nurse leaned over to look more closely. "It's not much of one, but using a little imagination, I would say it does qualify as a smile."

Margaret was laughing inside. She had prayed for just the right manager for the pharmacy. This was a far better solution than she could have dreamed of—and to think that Mrs. Simpson was thrown in as a bonus!

Thank You, Lord. What a wonderful surprise! You not

only heard me, but You did more than I asked for. Thank You.

A few weeks later Sally and Tom left. Margaret would miss them, but she knew they were doing what they felt called to do. So she was happy for them. In fact, she hadn't been this happy since the accident, except for the first time she had seen Heather Lynn.

Her mother visited regularly again. Her loneliness seemed to have lifted, and Margaret was relieved to see her old cheerfulness return.

Besides, no one could be depressed for long with Mrs. Simpson around.

The reading program had been reinstated. Occasionally, when Evelyn was unable to come or couldn't stay long, Mrs. Simpson substituted after working hours. Heather Lynn joined in too.

"Our house has sold," Mrs. Simpson announced one day. "We signed the contract last night to buy the Martins' house. It's not as large as our old house, but it's perfect for us now. We'll still have two extra bedrooms for the boys when they come to stay. Best of all, it's only four houses from your mother."

That's terrific! I'm glad you'll be so close to Mama. I know she's thrilled.

With the Simpsons settled in, a new activity was added to Margaret's increasingly busy schedule. One afternoon a week, according to Mrs. Simpson's day off, she and Evelyn would come to take her home for the day.

The weather was warming, and the pleasures of sitting on the old porch were unmatched. The warm breeze and the

———————CHOICES———————

sound of the birds brought back happy memories of romping across the broad lawn after Friskie. Here Margaret was free to run—if only in her imagination.

"Hi, Mommy!" Heather Lynn called, breaking into Margaret's daydreams. Always happy to be with her mother, the child skipped up the walk to the porch and kissed Margaret. She put her school bag down and gave her weekly report on school, friends and other activities. Mrs. Simpson would usually walk over then. She, Evelyn and Heather Lynn would return Margaret to the nursing home. Even before she was back in her room, Margaret was looking forward to her visit home the following week.

The warm weather passed. The home visits became less frequent with the arrival of the winter snows. Spring followed with its promises of renewal. And so it went year after year.

Sally and Tom came home. Their family was growing. Elizabeth had married the year before and had a son named Thomas Paul. Elias planned to get married while his parents were on furlough. Then they were off again for another three years.

Heather Lynn was entering high school. To Margaret's delight, the girl still did not see her mother as a burden or an embarrassment. She continued to be as attentive as ever.

On one bright fall day, when the leaves were at their height of color, Margaret waited impatiently for her mother and Mrs. Simpson to come for her. She was eager to breathe in the crisp fall air. But as the sun made its long, slow trip across the sky, still no one had come. The western sky broke into an explosion of sunset color, and then darkness set in.

Next morning Mrs. Simpson was back on the job. But she

seemed to go about her work in a solemn mood.

What's going on? Margaret wanted to ask. But Mrs. Simpson remained silent. In fact, she seemed to be avoiding her.

Something's wrong. Something is really wrong.

It wasn't until evening that Margaret's mother arrived alone. Her countenance was as sobering as Mrs. Simpson's. She pulled a chair up to Margaret's bed and sat quietly for a long time before speaking.

"Sweetheart, I'm sorry we couldn't get you yesterday. Things have been a little chaotic over the last few days. I'm afraid it's going to be a while before I can get back here to see you. I'll be going into the hospital tomorrow morning for surgery." She forced a smile. "The doctor found a suspicious lump, and he doesn't want to take any chances. Don't worry about me, dear. It's probably nothing at all, and I'll be as good as new in no time."

Mother, no! You don't fool me—I know you're scared. And this is serious, isn't it? I love you, Mama! Please be all right! Heather Lynn and I need you!

Margaret noticed how old and tired her mother had become. Why hadn't she seen it before?

God, You've heard me before, and You've answered my prayers so many times, even more than I've asked for. Please—I beg of You—don't let this be serious.

In the coming days she prayed intensely for her mother. Mrs. Simpson gave her regular reports on Mrs. Beaumont's progress. But it seemed as though she were hiding something.

Did the biopsy show cancer? Margaret was certain a biopsy would be a part of this kind of surgery, but not a word was spoken on the subject. That question remained foremost in her mind.

───────CHOICES───────

Mrs. Simpson, who was usually tuned in to Margaret's thoughts, seemed aloof.

One afternoon, as Margaret lay worrying over her mother, she overheard a frightening conversation. Two nurses were standing in the hall, just outside Margaret's door, speaking in low, urgent tones.

"So what do you think about the Supreme Court's decision?" one asked.

"I'm not sure. I guess we better brace ourselves for some action around here, though," the other said.

"Yeah, I've heard quite a few relatives have already inquired about the nursing home's release program. I figure about half our patients are eligible for termination. This could cost the health care industry a lot of jobs. I know the insurance companies and the welfare programs are probably thrilled with the new law, but I hope someone was watching out for us when it was passed."

Margaret strained to hear every word.

The first nurse was speaking again. "So do you think you'll participate if you get called on?"

"I don't know. I just don't know. It's one thing to pull the plug on a brain-dead patient, or even to withhold extreme medical procedures from the terminally ill and let nature take its course. But it's another matter entirely to deliberately end someone's life by a lethal injection. I don't know if I could do it."

"You just have to look at it as part of the job. It's perfectly legal. You shouldn't feel guilty about following through on someone else's decision. As far as I'm concerned, it's no different from the old abortion issue—it's not my decision, so it's not my responsibility."

O God, it's been passed and upheld by the Supreme Court! How can our nation allow this? So much for life, liberty and the pursuit of happiness. O God, dear God....

Another voice could now be heard in the hallway. It was the angry voice of Mrs. Simpson.

"What do you girls think you're doing, discussing this subject where some of the patients might hear you?"

"No one can hear us," one nurse said.

"No?" Mrs. Simpson continued. "If there's one thing I've learned over the years, it's that some patients can hear through walls. The lady in the wheelchair over there or the patients on the other side of this doorway might all be within earshot."

Margaret could hear the nurses leaving the area. Mrs. Simpson came into the room and checked her patients. Margaret was last.

"You heard that conversation, didn't you, girl? The whole thing makes me furious. How dare man abuse God's authority like that! One day God's going to run out of patience with this nation of ours.

"Oh, I wish you hadn't heard that talk. I don't want you worrying. You're one of the lucky ones. You've got family that loves you and won't let anything happen to you. Your mom's not taking any chances—she's already talked to the lawyer and made plans for your future if anything happens to her."

Mrs. Simpson changed Margaret's position, patted her on the hand and left. Margaret felt a little more secure, but she was no less upset that such a bill could be passed.

It was about a week later that Mrs. Reiner, the elderly woman in the next bed, had an unusually long parade of visitors. Margaret didn't know much about the woman but figured her condition was similar to her own. She never spoke and was never taken out. Her visitors had been few. Occasionally one of her four children stopped by, but they never stayed long. Now this large company had suddenly descended upon Mrs. Reiner.

Strange, Margaret thought. This has all the trappings of a birthday party. But her birthday was last month. What's going on?

The older daughter entered first, carrying a bouquet of white flowers. She kissed the old woman, then stepped back to allow her husband and children to follow. The younger daughter came in, also carrying a bouquet. Then it was the sons' turns. Nieces, nephews and family friends joined the parade.

Abruptly, Mrs. Simpson burst into the room and pulled the curtains on either side of Mrs. Reiner's bed. She was upset and made no effort to conceal the fact.

It's not a birthday party, Margaret realized with horror. It's more like a death-day party! Poor Mrs. Reiner. I hope she's not aware of what's going on. This is horrible!

Margaret shuddered inwardly as each visitor took his turn saying good-bye. One by one they passed by the foot of Margaret's bed as they left. Many of them dabbed their eyes as they went by.

Margaret's stomach was in knots.

Heather Lynn caught a ride to the nursing home from a neighbor that day. She came in as soon as the last visitor had left. She wore a puzzled look on her face.

"Hi, Mom. I've been here for a while, but Mrs. Simpson wouldn't let me come in until all those people left. I don't know what's going on, but is she ever upset!"

Thank God for Mrs. Simpson! It's just as well you don't know what's going on.

"Well, anyway, she took me to see Grandma last night, but she probably already told you about that. I think Grandma's doing much better and will be coming home soon.

I sure do miss her. Mrs. Simpson's been taking good care of me, but I'm sure anxious to go home and sleep in my own bed.''

So you're staying with the Simpsons, are you? Is there nothing they wouldn't do for us?

"Aunt Jessica was here a few days ago, but I tried to keep my distance. We were all glad when she left. She always upsets everyone. Mrs. Simpson was angry with her for something she said to Grandma. She was almost as angry as she is today."

I can just imagine what my dear sister said. It was probably something like, "Mom, don't you think it's about time to rescue poor Margaret from her misery? Just think of all the money we'd save."

"Well, Mom, I suppose it's been a while since you've been read to," Heather Lynn said.

The girl opened the dresser drawer and took out the current book. She read for about half an hour before Mrs. Simpson came in and told her it was time to go home.

As they were about to leave, Althea suddenly turned and spoke quietly. "Margaret, don't let anything disturb you tonight. Keep your peace, and call upon the good Lord if you get upset."

What does she mean by that? But then Margaret remembered old Mrs. Reiner in the next bed.

Sometime during the night two nurses entered the room with a stretcher. They pulled the curtains. A few minutes later they wheeled Mrs. Reiner out of the room. Margaret swallowed hard, knowing she would never see the woman again.

Within the hour one of the nurse's aides came in and stripped the bed. She gathered up Mrs. Reiner's personal possessions.

Waves of nausea swept over Margaret.

I can't believe this is happening! It's so easy—hardly any effort at all to take a life. This law certainly does make it convenient. I can see where a whole new set of funeral customs will evolve. It is now possible to plan a funeral for a convenient time and then arrange the death for the night before. Very neat, indeed!

Although plagued with the horror of this atrocity, Margaret was exhausted from the emotions of the day, and she soon slipped into sleep.

---————TWELVE———---

I<small>T WAS A THIN, FRAIL WOMAN WHO</small> accompanied Mrs. Simpson to Margaret's room one afternoon. Evelyn Beaumont leaned heavily on her friend's arm as she entered the room.

No, it can't be! Mama? Yes, it is! But what's happened to her? She looks terrible!

Althea placed a chair next to the bed, helped Evelyn into it and left the room.

"It was a bit more serious than we thought," Margaret's mother said. "I should be all right now. I'm still weak, but the doctor assures me that it will pass. He thinks he got all the cancer, but I've been receiving chemotherapy just to be sure."

Margaret wanted so badly to reach out to her mother.

O, God, please let her be all right. She looks awful.

─────────────── C H O I C E S ───────────────

Make her better real soon.

"As usual, Althea's been so helpful. I know I sound repetitious, but I don't know what we'd do without her and George.

"Your brother's due home in two months. Even though I feel confident about getting better, he insists upon taking his furlough early."

That makes me feel better.

"I want you to know that I've started to make provision for you and Heather Lynn should anything happen to me. Everything will be finalized as soon as Tom gets home."

Don't talk like that, Mama! I couldn't bear to lose you.

Margaret was certain her eyes betrayed her panic, but her mother didn't respond.

"I'm going to sign over half the pharmacy to the Simpsons. The other half will be held in trust for you and Heather Lynn. If I do that now, I'll be assured that Jessica won't get involved with the pharmacy and cut off your support. It's terrible to say this about my own daughter, but I just don't trust her."

Believe me, I'm glad you don't. Neither do I.

"The business has become very profitable over the past few years—especially over the short time George has managed it. It should bring in enough income to cover your expenses, providing costs don't go up too high. I can manage on the income my properties generate. Everything else will be divided equally between the four of you when I'm gone. I'm including Heather Lynn since she's been as close as any daughter could be—and, of course, she has her trust fund.

"I'm hoping I can find some way to keep the house in the family. I've got some ideas, but I'll talk to Tom about them when he gets home."

I wonder what Jessica will think of all this.

"I think I've learned a little of what you must feel. As I was convalescing, I tried to imagine what it must be like for you day after day. I know it's not only difficult, but very frustrating. I just wish I could do more for you, dear."

Mom, you've done more than anyone else would have in your shoes. I'm grateful for everything you've done, and I couldn't expect anything more.

Her mother was sitting quietly now, stroking Margaret's hand. Mrs. Simpson came in.

"Evelyn, I think I'd better be getting you home. I don't want you to collapse from exhaustion on your first day out."

"I know you're right, but I really don't want to go quite yet, Althea."

It's all right, Mama. I wouldn't defy Nurse Simpson if I were you. I've never known her not to get her way.

Evelyn Beaumont patted her daughter's hand and smiled warmly. "I guess I'd better go. The sooner I get my strength back, the sooner I can visit on my own without having to deal with Althea's bossiness!"

"I'll bring her back again real soon, if she behaves herself," Althea promised.

Althea helped her friend up from the chair and supported her as they left.

Margaret was greatly encouraged by her mother's next few visits. The color was returning to her face, and except for the loss of hair, she seemed to be almost back to normal.

When Mrs. Beaumont seemed to be in good health again, Tom and Sally returned to the mission field with confidence.

―――――――― CHOICES ――――――――

They had been gone only a month when Margaret detected her mother's health slipping again. Within a few weeks she was back in the hospital.

Mrs. Simpson had been absent from work for several days. Finally one afternoon she came to see Margaret, her eyes puffy from crying. She sat quietly, holding Margaret's hand.

Mrs. Simpson, please say something. Is it my mother? Has she died? What's made you so upset? Please, tell me!

"I'm sorry for coming in here like this, girl," Althea said. "I hope I'm not upsetting you, but I've just got to talk to somebody. I've tried to be there for you and your mom for many years, and now I just need for you to hear me out."

Fine. It's about time I could do something for you, even if it is just lying here and listening.

"I love your mom like a sister. You know I'd never do anything to hurt her or take advantage of her. Margaret, your mom is real sick. We won't have her with us much longer, and all I want is for her to have peace in her final days. Girl, she deserves it! She doesn't deserve to be caught up in Jessica's mess."

So that's it—Jessica!

Althea stood up and paced about the bed. "That sister of yours accused me today of befriending your folks just to get at their money. She says she's going after us as soon as your mother passes away. She's already got a lawyer looking into getting the family business back."

Althea slammed her right fist into her left hand. "I can't believe that woman! What your mother and I have done for each other has been out of love. I don't think Jessica has any idea what that means. I'll not allow something so beautiful to be turned into something dirty."

It's a good thing I can't move, or I'd be repenting of murder before morning. God, forgive me, but if I were physically able, I think I would wring Jessica's neck!

Althea was still pacing. "When I said she'd hurt your mother terribly if she continued to challenge her wishes, she said I needn't worry since she wouldn't do anything until Evelyn was beyond knowing anything. She also said it might be sooner than anyone expects since she, as the only next-of-kin around, would not allow her mother to suffer long when relief was available."

Surely she's not thinking about....

Althea looked squarely at Margaret. "I asked Jessica if she intended to invoke the mercy-killing law. She just smiled and walked away."

She is thinking about it! What is wrong with that sister of mine? Has she gone completely crazy? I knew she could be vicious, but I never thought she'd go this far. How on earth could Mother have two such opposite children as Jessica and Tom?

"Well, I had enough of her threats." Althea sat down again and drew up close. "I figured if she tried to do anything, and Tom weren't around, nobody would be able to stop her. I had asked her earlier if she'd contacted Tom. Her answer was vague so I assumed she hadn't. I hope I did the right thing, but I went over Jessica's head and sent a telegram to Tom. I told him your mom was seriously ill and he should come home as soon as possible."

You did the right thing. Tom is the only one who can control Jessica. Since he has the power of attorney, he should be here anyway.

"Margaret, I was so angry! I just had to get out of that hospital and away from that sister of yours. I knew if I stayed around another minute, I'd do something I'd regret later. I got in the car, sent the telegram and, without really thinking, I drove over here."

Althea Simpson quietly reached out and took Margaret's hand again. She was crying.

Lord, Margaret prayed silently, comfort this dear woman. Restore her peace of mind, and strengthen her in the days to come. Be with my dear mother, and don't let her be upset by Jessica. And please, please—bring Tom home quickly!

In two weeks Tom and Sally returned home. Mrs. Simpson came to work the next morning lighter in spirit—humming once again.

"God bless that brother of yours!" Althea said as she took Margaret's blood pressure. "George and I picked Sally and Tom up at the airport last night. You should have seen Jessica's face when they walked into the house. Whee! Was she ever surprised! Heather Lynn was delighted to see them, but your sister was obviously upset."

I can imagine.

"She went on about their insensitivity for not having informed her of their coming. Tom was so gracious. He said he was glad I had contacted them, because her communication evidently got lost enroute. They were sure Jessica would be expecting them since he didn't think for a minute that she wouldn't have sent for them. She didn't say much after that, but did she ever give me a dirty look!"

Althea made some notations and then removed the blood pressure cuff. "Well, you're healthy enough today."

She continued. "Tom certainly doesn't stand for any of Jessica's nonsense. He straightened me out too. I have a much better perspective on things now that I'm praying for Jessica and not allowing my anger to get the best of me."

I'm praying for her too, but she only seems to be getting worse. It's helped me, but I must confess I'm still pretty mad at her.

"Tom and Sally are at the hospital right now. They said they'd be around to see you later today.

"You can't imagine how relieved I am to have them back. I didn't like Heather Lynn staying in the house alone with Jessica all this time. Who knows what that woman might tell her? Well, now we can relax. Heather Lynn's out from under Jessica's influence, and the whole situation is in Tom's hands."

She moved on to the other woman in the room.

I'm relieved too, Mrs. Simpson. I'll sleep much better now that Tom's home.

Sally and Tom arrived in the late afternoon. The moment Margaret saw them, a wave of peace and confidence swept over her.

"Hello, sis." Tom bent down, gave Margaret a kiss and moved the lounge chair away from the window. "They treating you all right?"

As well as can be expected.

Sally kissed her and sat down on the edge of the bed. "We saw Mom today. She was very weak, but glad to see us."

Tom pulled a chair up to Margaret's chair and sat down. "We got home just as fast as we could. There was so much to do before we left the mission. Our co-workers were left with the bulk of the packing and shipping. We're not going back, Margaret—at least not for a long time. We both feel we need to be here on a more permanent basis. Someone's got to take charge, and I don't think Jessica's the one for the job."

You're right there!

"Not knowing how things will go for Mom," Sally said, "we've decided to move into the house. That way we'll be able to keep an eye on Heather Lynn and help out if Mom does come home. Jessica seems more than eager to leave now that we're back."

"Jessica wants to take Heather Lynn home with her," Tom said, "but that is, of course, out of the question. We'd never allow it. Mom made it clear we would become Heather Lynn's guardians should anything happen to her. We never expected things to turn out this way, but nevertheless we're glad to care for Heather Lynn. She's a lovely young lady and seems to be doing well in spite of everything that's going on. You can certainly be proud of her."

I am!

Sally got up and took the hairbrush from the nightstand. She stood in back of Margaret and brushed her hair as Tom continued.

"Every time I've come home, Dr. Anderson has asked me to join his practice. He's a man I think I could work with. He's nearing retirement now, so it may be a possibility. I'm going to talk to him tonight."

I hope things work out for you. I know it's a sacrifice for both of you to come home, and I'm grateful for all you're doing. It's not easy leaving your life's work behind. If it were just me, I'd want you to go back to the mission. But Heather Lynn and Mama need you right now. Heather Lynn's been through so much turmoil in her short life that I know she's going to need your influence. There's no one else for her. I certainly don't want her exposed to Jessica any longer than necessary.

Tom spoke again. "Mother wanted me to arrange for you to be brought to the hospital. I hope you won't mind, but it's her deepest desire to see you."

What does that mean? Won't she be leaving the hospital again to come and visit me here?

"As soon as I can make the arrangements, I'll come for you," he said.

As Sally and Tom left that day, Margaret felt a sense of foreboding. Although Sally mentioned the possibility of Evelyn's going home, the request for a visit from Margaret and the tone of Tom's voice indicated finality. Margaret could hardly stand the pain that pierced her heart at the thought of losing her mother. She cried within herself for the remainder of the day and long into the night.

Three days later Margaret was wheeled into the hospital room where her mother lay. Tom and Sally placed the wheelchair as close to her mother's bedside as possible and left the room.

"Oh, Margaret, dear. I'm so glad you're here."

Mama, you look terrible!

Margaret's worst suspicions were confirmed. Any flicker of hope for her mother's recovery fled.

"It's strange to have you visit me. It's been the other way around for so many years. I hope you don't mind being brought here, but I had to see you one more time."

One more time? Then you think it's going to be soon?

Evelyn's voice grew weaker with each word. "I wanted to tell you how much I love you, and what a joy Heather Lynn has been to me. It was that sweet child who brought me through many a dark time. A day hasn't passed that I haven't thanked God for giving your father and me the strength to refuse the abortion. I want to ask your forgiveness for any pain we may have caused you in that decision, but I hope you now understand why. There's no telling how you feel about it all."

Mama, you're forgiven. I wish I could tell you what I wanted to tell Daddy when he talked with me before he died—I forgave you the moment I saw Heather Lynn.

"There's one more thing, dear. I...I certainly hope you're understanding this. If you haven't already, please, please, make your peace with God. We haven't been able to communicate with each other for so long, but it doesn't have to be that way forever. It's my greatest desire for us to be together in the next life, where such barriers don't exist."

Evelyn Beaumont's voice was failing. She closed her eyes and dozed off for a few minutes before continuing.

"I don't want to be parted from you or Jessica for eternity. If you can pray, please, pray for your sister. As much trouble as she has been to all of us, I still love her."

I guess I do too, though I still get pretty upset with her.

"My dear Margaret, I worry about you so. I wish there were some way of knowing what you're thinking."

Margaret could see her mother grimacing in pain.

Mama, I wish I could put your mind at peace about me, but I guess I'll have to rely on the Lord to do that. I'll be fine.

"Don't you worry about me. I'm going to a far better place. In fact, now that Tom's home, I'm eager to go. I miss your father so, and I know I'll be with him again soon. We'll both be waiting for you when your time comes."

Evelyn smiled warmly and caressed Margaret's cheek with her thin, trembling hand. "I love you," she whispered.

I love you, too, Mama.

Margaret sat, strapped in her wheelchair. She watched as her mother slipped back into sleep. She knew this was the last time she would see her mother alive. These last quiet moments at her bedside were precious, and Margaret hoped Tom and Sally wouldn't return for a long while.

We'll both be just fine, Mama. Just fine.

Sally and Tom rejoined Margaret in the hospital room. They kissed the sleeping woman good-bye and returned Margaret to the nursing home. Just as they reached the doorway to her room, Margaret's roommate was pushed out on a stretcher. The woman was still, staring up at the ceiling. A nurse was already stripping the bed and packing up personal belongings.

"Althea mentioned that Margaret's roommate would be taken some time today," Sally whispered to Tom as they waited in the hallway. "It's just horrible what they're doing."

"Well, it's not going to happen to anyone in my family!" Tom said. "I'm so grateful Mother had the foresight to arrange for Margaret's expenses. I'll pay the health care costs out of my own pocket or take care of her myself before I'll be forced into that!"

Margaret took comfort from Tom's words. She trusted him and knew she had people around her who took responsibility for one another. Except Jessica, of course. But she wouldn't have much say about anything as long as Tom was around.

A week later Tom stood by Margaret's bedside. It was very late—not the usual time for a visit.

"Margaret," he said, "Mother has gone to be with Father."

THIRTEEN

FOLLOWING THE FUNERAL, MARGARET'S life changed radically. One morning a new nurse entered the room and opened the blinds. It was Althea's day to work, but this new nurse had evidently taken over her duties. Margaret listened carefully, straining to detect her friend's voice in the corridor.

It was no secret that Althea Simpson was having trouble with the nursing home officials because of her refusal to participate in the release program. Could she have been fired? Or had she quit rather than take part in what she considered murder?

She didn't say anything about leaving, Margaret thought. It must have been sudden. What will I ever do without her?

Margaret was tottering on the brink of panic.

──────────── CHOICES ────────────

The nurse's aide spent more time than usual giving Margaret her bath and attending to her appearance. For a moment Margaret entertained the thought that she was being prepared for the kill. She dismissed the idea, knowing her family would never allow it.

Maybe they're preparing me to go out today. But no one mentioned an outside visit. What's going on?

"There you are, pretty as a picture," the nurse's aide said.

Margaret was strapped into the wheelchair and pushed in front of the window. From there she could see the broad front lawn and the long, circular drive. A familiar car was just turning into it.

That's Tom's car. I must be going on a home visit.

Soon she heard footsteps approaching her door.

"Hi, Mom," Heather Lynn said. She kissed her mother and turned the wheelchair around.

Tom and Sally were standing in the doorway. They were smiling.

"Well, are you going to tell her?" Tom asked.

Heather Lynn moved to the front of the wheelchair and knelt down. "Mom, we're taking you home today. For *good*. You're going to live with us from now on."

How can this be? You're kidding, aren't you?

"It's true," Tom said. "We've gone over our finances with an accountant. Since you're on the 'cancellation list,' you're no longer eligible for insurance benefits or public assistance. Mom left money to pay for your expenses, but it's going to have to last a long time. We figure it'll only cost us half as much to take care of you at home.

"Mrs. Simpson has been wanting to get out of the nursing home for some time. She's refused to assist in the so-called 'release program,' so she figured it was just a matter of time before she got fired. She was thrilled when we proposed that she come to work for us. With her help, we feel confident about bringing you home. Sally's a nurse, I'm a doctor—why, we've got our own team!"

"And don't forget me," Heather Lynn added. "I'm going to do my share."

To think that after all these years I'll actually be living under the same roof with my daughter. I can't believe it!

"We've spent the last few weeks fixing up the downstairs bedroom," Sally said. "It has everything you need."

"I hope you like it, Mom," Heather Lynn said. "It was my job to pick out the wallpaper and the paint and the curtains."

I'm sure I'm going to love it. Let's not stay here another second! I'm going home!

Althea was waiting on the porch as the car turned into the driveway. The arrival felt like a celebration, and Margaret was certain they could all hear her laughing with joy as they wheeled her into the house. She had long since given up hope of this ever happening. Yet, here she was, at home—and not for just a few hours, but for as long as she lived.

The familiar creak in the hall floor welcomed her as the wheelchair passed over. The tick-tock of the old grandfather clock greeted her from the corner of the living room, where it had stood for four generations.

As Sally had said, Margaret's new room lacked for nothing. Even with all the hospital equipment, the room had been made cozy and homey. Opposite the bed was an entertainment center with a color television and a small stereo. Flowered wallpaper graced the walls, and perky pink curtains framed the windows. Over the bed was the very picture that had hung above Margaret's bed when she was a child—a print of a little girl running through a field of wildflowers.

You did a good job with the wallpaper and curtains, Heather Lynn. It's exactly what I would have chosen. I wonder if taste is hereditary.

Heather Lynn picked up a vase of wildflowers from the nightstand and held them up for Margaret to see. "I picked these this morning."

What a lovely bouquet! Thank you, my dear daughter.

Instead of putting Margaret in the hospital bed, Tom lifted her from the wheelchair and placed her in a comfortable recliner near the double windows. From there she could see across the lawn to the next-door neighbor's house and the street beyond. Several children wheeled past on bicycles. The neighbor let her puppy out. There was activity everywhere.

Tom set the chair in a comfortable position, then joined the others in the kitchen for lunch. The aroma of beef stew and hot cornbread spilled into Margaret's room, as did the cheery conversation.

"She seems comfortable enough," Tom said.

"I just can't believe my mother's home," Heather Lynn said.

"Well, she is, and you can go in and see her anytime you want," Sally said. "Now let's say the blessing and eat."

Margaret could hear Tom praying. "Lord, this is, indeed, a special day. Thank You for making it possible to bring Margaret home. We acknowledge You as our source and strength in all things. Thank You for this food. May it strengthen our bodies so we are better able to serve You today. Amen."

―――――――CHOICES―――――――

"Amen," came a chorus from around the table.
I want to thank You, too, Lord. It's so good to be home.

Althea was completing Margaret's daily routine of passive exercises. She replaced Margaret's hand splints and adjusted them for comfort.

"It's too nice a day to stay inside," she said. "How about a walk?"

Sounds great.

"I'll be in to help you as soon as I get the chili in the crock pot," Sally called from the kitchen.

Althea started the preparations for the outing. Sally came in and took her position for Margaret's transfer from the bed to the wheelchair.

"One, two, three, lift," Mrs. Simpson said. "Good. It's a good thing you're a lightweight, Margaret. I'm not getting any younger."

Sally buckled the straps and wheeled Margaret to the front porch. The newly installed ramp made the trip from the porch to the sidewalk effortless.

"Hello, Rose," Althea called.

"Good morning, Althea, Sally," the next-door neighbor replied. She watched with interest as they passed.

The warmth of the morning sun, here and there interrupted by the cool shadows of the maples and oaks that lined the street, felt good on Margaret's skin. A gentle breeze stirred the leaves.

The mailman approached them on his rounds. "Good morning, ladies. Lovely day, isn't it?"

"It certainly is—one of those days you dream of in January," Althea said.

CHOICES

The mailman chuckled. "You've got that right, Mrs. Simpson."

They were now in front of the Simpsons' house. Althea went up to her door, opened the mailbox and quickly scanned the envelopes to see if there was anything of interest. She picked out one, opened it and read it silently.

"I don't believe this," she said when she finished.

"Jessica again?" Sally asked.

"Her lawyer."

Althea handed the letter to Sally. She read it and handed it back. "She won't give up, will she?"

What? What's Jessica up to now?

But no further explanation was given. Althea shook her head in dismay as she took the pile of mail into the house. She returned, and they resumed the walk.

As pleasant as the walk had been, Margaret was disturbed knowing Mrs. Simpson was still the target of Jessica's attacks.

I just wonder how far she will go.

FOURTEEN

IT WOULD SOON BE TIME FOR HEATHER Lynn to return home from school—the best part of the day as far as Margaret was concerned. She sat in the recliner, watching out the window. She usually preferred to sit on the porch and wait, but today was damp and dreary, making the porch uninviting.

At last Heather Lynn came into sight. She stopped and patted the energetic puppy from the house next door. She then shooed the puppy back toward its own house and cut across the grass.

"I'm home, Aunt Sally," Margaret could hear her call from the front hall.

"I'm upstairs," Sally answered. "I'll be down in a little while. Take it easy on the chocolate chip cookies. They're for the bake sale tomorrow."

―――――――――― CHOICES ――――――――――

"Don't worry. I'll try just one. I have to watch my figure, you know."

The thud of Heather Lynn's books echoed down the hallway. Soon the girl appeared in the doorway, cookie in hand.

"Hi, Mom," she said, plopping down across Margaret's bed.

How was your day, dear?

"Mmmm, this is good." She downed the rest of the cookie. "It was a pretty good day. I got back my history test. I got a ninety-six."

That's good.

"I would have had a hundred, but I made a stupid mistake."

A ninety-six isn't bad. I wouldn't complain if I were you.

Heather Lynn was staring at her mother. "Mom, I know I've said this before, but it's just so good having you around. Do you realize that I'm the only senior girl who has a mother who listens to her? All the others complain that their mothers don't have time for them. I definitely don't have *that* problem. I tell them that my mom not only has time for me, but she never interrupts me. You know, they envy me."

Yes, listening is something I do very well.

"Well, anyway, you'll never guess what I found out today."

You're right, I'll never guess.

"Jimmy Chapman and Stephanie Wagner broke up over the weekend. Word is, he's going to ask me to the homecoming dance. Can you believe it? Mom, he's gorgeous! He's also rich—owns his own car."

I suppose that's good news, but I trust your uncle will have

136

something to say about it. It seems to me I remember your saying something about this Jimmy Chapman being a little on the wild side.

"I'll definitely have to get a new outfit. I saw just what I want at the mall when I was down there last Saturday. If he does ask me, I'll take some money out of the bank and get it. It's pretty expensive, but I couldn't wear anything cheap if I go out with Jimmy Chapman."

Heather Lynn got up from the bed and started for the door. "I'll get changed, grab my homework and be back in a jiff." A few minutes later she was back. As she did almost every afternoon, she spread her books out on the floor and went to work.

"Heather Lynn, your uncle's home," Sally called from the kitchen. "You can set the table now."

"I'll be right there as soon as I finish this problem."

A few minutes later, she gathered up her books and went to the kitchen, where she set the table while Sally put the finishing touches on dinner.

In the meantime, Tom came into Margaret's room and gave her a quick examination before wheeling her into the kitchen. Margaret still relied upon the feeding tube for her sustenance, but it had become routine to have her join the family around the supper table.

"Have you heard from Althea today?" Tom asked his wife. "Is her life getting back to normal?"

Sally passed the meatloaf.

"Yes, she called me this afternoon. Her son and his family left shortly after lunch. She said she'd be over tomorrow morning as soon as she gets the house back in order."

"No doubt you'll be getting an earful about the grandchildren."

———————— CHOICES ————————

"No doubt," Sally said. "I've certainly talked enough about mine. I hope I can be as gracious with her as she's been with me."

Heather Lynn laughed. "Did you see what the little one did after church yesterday?" She reached for the mashed potatoes.

"No," Sally replied. "What did I miss?"

"Well, you know that Miss Cummings? Always sits in the second row on the left side? The one who always wears the big hats?"

I sure do, Margaret thought. She completely ignores me. The way she holds her nose up in the air, she probably doesn't even see me.

"Well, she was cooing at little Sarah when suddenly the baby threw up all over her. You should have seen her face. I had to do everything I could not to laugh." She passed the potatoes to Tom, who was chuckling at the thought of Miss Cummings's discomfiture.

"It's not right to laugh," Sally objected. "Poor Miss Cummings—she must have been mortified." There was a pause while Tom and Heather Lynn tried to put on a straight face. "Please, pass the corn," Sally said.

The telephone rang, and Heather Lynn jumped up to answer it. She stepped into Margaret's room to talk.

Margaret was still laughing inside—not because of Miss Cummings's predicament, but because of the stern look on Sally's face.

"Do you want gravy, Tom?" she asked.

Tom regained his composure. "Yes, please. Any messages for me?"

"Yes, one—Pastor DiAngelo wants you to call him sometime this evening. He wants to talk to you about the retreat next month."

Heather Lynn burst into the kitchen. "Guess who that was!"

I bet it was Jimmy Chapman, Margaret thought.

"Haven't the foggiest," Tom said.

"It was Jimmy Chapman. He asked me to go to the homecoming dance with him next Friday."

Heather Lynn's announcement wasn't met with the enthusiasm she had hoped for. Her smile faded.

"What did you tell him?" Tom asked.

"I told him I'd love to go, but I'd have to check with you and Aunt Sally first."

"Good. What are the details?"

"I guess he'll come and get me, take me to the dance, and bring me home."

"Will he be driving?" Sally asked.

"I suppose so. He has his own car."

Sally thought for a moment. "Is this the same Jimmy Chapman who was arrested last summer for driving under the influence of alcohol?"

"How did you know about that?"

"Never mind how, I just know."

"I suppose that means you're not going to let me go."

"I wouldn't say that," Tom said, "but we do have to take that into consideration. We love you, Heather Lynn. We wouldn't want to put you into a dangerous situation. Your Aunt Sally and I will discuss it and let you know."

Give it careful consideration, Tom. I haven't been comfortable with the idea since Heather Lynn first brought it up.

Heather Lynn came into Margaret's room and threw herself into the recliner. She stared at the blank television screen for a few minutes, picked up the remote control, flicked it a few times and turned it off again. She spun around in the chair and looked in her mother's direction.

"I don't believe this!" she said. "Here it is, the night of the homecoming dance, and I'm sitting home. Aunt Sally and Uncle Tom said I couldn't go to the dance with Jimmy Chapman because of his reputation—they don't think he's responsible. Aunt Sally said when I'm eighteen I can start making my own decisions, but for now I have to follow *their* rules. I told her *you* wouldn't be so old-fashioned. Would you, Mom?"

Oh, yes, I would. I'd probably be more strict with you than Aunt Sally is. I suspect I've had more first-hand knowledge of the dangers out there than she has.

"I just can't believe I'm missing the dance! And what makes it worse is that Jimmy's taking Lori Braden instead of me. She's supposed to be my best friend. How could she go with him when she knew how upset I was? How could Aunt Sally and Uncle Tom do this to me? Jimmy's one of the most popular guys in school. He has his own car, and is he ever cute! And here I sit, missing the best opportunity of my high school career." She crossed her arms angrily.

My dear child, Margaret thought, it seems so important to you now, but it's really not the end of the world. There will be many other special occasions, and many more Jimmys. You'll get over this one disappointment.

Heather Lynn sighed and turned back to the television, which she flicked on again. She spoke very little for the rest of the evening and went to bed early.

Margaret heard the telephone ring in the middle of the night. Moments later Tom came down the stairs and rushed out the back door.

─────────────── CHOICES ───────────────

Another emergency call, Margaret thought, and fell back to sleep.

Heather Lynn slept in late, as she always did on Saturday morning. It was almost 11:00 before she made her appearance in Margaret's room, balancing a bowl of cereal and a glass of orange juice. She plopped down on the recliner and switched on the television.

"Good morning, Mom."

Good morning, dear. Are you feeling better this morning?

"I guess Uncle Tom's having quite a time. The police called him around 2:00 this morning, and he isn't home yet. I bet he's exhausted. Aunt Sally said it was some car accident on the interstate."

Heather Lynn became engrossed with her cereal and the television program. It was almost noon before Tom returned. Margaret could hear him speaking with Sally in the kitchen, but the television drowned out their words.

He appeared in the doorway, disheveled. Blood stains covered his shirt and jacket. Sally stood behind him, wiping her eyes.

"Turn off the television, Heather Lynn. I have to talk to you," Tom said.

She flicked it off.

"Honey, there was an accident last night."

"I know." Heather Lynn was puzzled.

"Your friend Jimmy Chapman was driving. He was drunk. He crossed over the divider into the oncoming lane and hit a truck head on."

"Oh, no!" Heather Lynn stood, knocking her soggy cereal onto the floor. "Is he all right?"

"No, honey. He died two hours ago."

Margaret looked on helplessly as her daughter broke into hysterical crying. Tom went to her and held her a

141

long time before she was able to speak.

"What about Lori?"

"She was killed instantly. It took them almost all night to free her body from the wreckage."

Heather Lynn was again engulfed in anguish.

Lord Jesus, that could have been Heather Lynn! Thank You for Tom and Sally's wisdom.

And, Lord, please comfort the Chapmans and the Bradens. I'm overjoyed at Heather Lynn's being spared. But they're mourning the loss of their children. Hold them close and strengthen them through this terrible tragedy.

Tom was still holding Heather Lynn tightly. "There was another couple with them—Nancy Green and Bobby Romano. He's unconscious and in critical condition. The girl had her seatbelt on and was spared any injuries to the head, but she did lose her right leg. She was still in surgery when I left the hospital."

"Nancy's leg is being amputated?"

"Yes, dear, it wasn't possible to save it." Tom stroked her hair.

"What about the truck driver?" Sally asked.

"He had only minor injuries, but he's in pretty bad shape emotionally."

Heather Lynn sank down in the recliner. Sally sat on the arm of the chair and placed her hand on the girl's shoulder as she continued to cry.

"I can't believe any of this," she sobbed. "I just saw all of them in school yesterday. Now two of them are dead, and the other two are seriously injured. How could this have happened?"

"There are no easy answers to that question," Tom said. "None of us can even pretend to understand. All we can do is pray for the two who are still alive and all of their families.

———————CHOICES———————

They're going to need all the support they can get."

Suddenly, Heather Lynn stopped crying and looked up with wide, frantic eyes. "It should have been *me!* *I* should have died—not Lori!"

Sally drew the girl closer. "No, no, dear. You were doing exactly what you were supposed to be doing last night. Your obedience kept you safe. It was our concern for your safety that made us say you couldn't go out with Jimmy. Don't take on guilt that doesn't belong to you. You didn't do anything wrong. You're not responsible for Lori's death."

"But I should have been there, not Lori."

"*No*, Heather Lynn," Tom said firmly. "If you're so certain you were destined to die, then how do you explain the fact that you didn't?"

Heather Lynn said no more. She sobbed softly while Tom, exhausted both physically and emotionally, made his way upstairs to sleep.

Margaret was jolted out of her sleep by the slam of the storm door. Heather Lynn would be on her way to school. Margaret could hear Sally in the kitchen, pouring Tom a second cup of coffee.

"Tom, I'm really worried about her," she said.

"She's probably still upset about the accident. It's going to take time. We've got to leave room for her to mourn."

"How much time is she going to need? Do you realize it's been over two months? She hasn't shown any improvement at all. If anything, she gets worse every day. She's either sitting silently with Margaret or upstairs in her room alone. Did you know she doesn't go out with her friends anymore? She doesn't even talk on the phone."

"Now *there's* reason to be concerned," Tom chuckled.

"Tom, this is nothing to joke about. Heather Lynn needs help."

"I'm sorry. I guess I'm frustrated just like you, and I don't know what to do either. I'm not a psychiatrist, or a miracle worker." He threw his hands up in the air.

"It's just that she's so changed since the accident. I keep waiting for the old Heather Lynn to return, but she never does. I'm afraid she never will. She's so withdrawn, Tom. She's buried herself in her studies."

"Maybe we should try to talk with her again. Not that my last few attempts have done any good. Maybe at dinner tonight," he said.

"If you don't think it would be too upsetting for Margaret."

"Well, it may upset her, but I guess she's as concerned about her daughter as we are."

You're right there. I am just as concerned as you two are, but I can't do anything about it except pray.

Dinner was particularly quiet. Margaret had been brought to the table as usual. She waited for Tom to open the conversation. She could see Tom and Sally exchange looks several times, but nothing was said. It wasn't until Heather Lynn asked to be excused from the table that Tom finally brought up the subject.

"No, I'd rather have you stay a while. There's something we'd like to discuss with you."

Heather Lynn sat back down in her chair, a defiant look on her face. "What did I do wrong this time?"

"Nothing, dear," Sally assured her. "We're just concerned about you. We wondered if there was anything we could do to help you out of this depression you're in." Sally took her niece's hand.

Heather Lynn snapped her hand back. "I'm fine."

"Well, that's not exactly how we see it," Tom said.

"So you're a psychiatrist now, are you?"

"Heather Lynn, you've changed so drastically since the accident that we've really become concerned. At a time when you should be enjoying new experiences and making new friends, you've isolated yourself. You never call any of your friends, and as far as I know they never call you either."

"So? I'm just enjoying home. Is there anything wrong with that?" She stood up. "Can I go study?"

"No, sit down!" Tom said. "I want to understand."

Heather Lynn plopped back down in the chair. She stared at her plate.

Please, Heather Lynn, let us in.

The tension gave way as the girl burst into tears. She buried her face in her hands for several minutes, then turned toward her mother. "I just don't understand how a loving God could have done this! First He paralyzes my mother—before I was even born. Then He takes my grandfather and my grandmother. Then He takes my friends—one who died in my place. I feel guilty for even being alive. What have I done that's so terrible? Why does God want to punish me so?"

Oh, how I wish I could talk to you now!

Sally took Heather Lynn's hand. "Sweetheart, God's not punishing you. None of us is free from life's tragedies. True, you've had more troubles than most people your age, but God hasn't abandoned you. I know it's all very perplexing right now. Maybe we'll never fully understand the reasons in this life. But someday you'll know. To never experience difficulty or pain would leave us shallow individuals who

CHOICES

could never appreciate the good things that come our way every day."

"It's easy for you to think that. You're not in my shoes."

Sally didn't reply right away. She stood up and walked to the window. "You know I was orphaned at eleven when my parents were killed in an auto accident."

"Yes."

"Well, maybe you didn't know they were killed by a drunk driver in the middle of the afternoon—a time when you'd think you'd be safe from such things. It was election day, and they had left me to play with a friend while they went to vote, less than a mile away." Sally turned around and fixed her gaze on Heather Lynn. "Believe me, I've asked all the questions you're asking now. None of it made sense to me. It would have been so easy for me to be with them. I asked myself why I was spared. The only thing I could come up with over the years was that God had something for me to do. That's when I decided to become a nurse and go to the mission field. The older I get, the more I seem to understand. I'm sure you'll find the same thing true in your case."

"Yeah, sure!" Heather Lynn lowered her eyes to the tabletop. "At least *you* know who your father *was*."

Oh, Heather Lynn! Are you hurting that much?

Tom pulled himself closer, then reached out and lifted Heather Lynn's chin until her eyes met his. "I think you're reacting with a lot of self-pity, young lady."

She pushed his hand away. "Am I? Just think about it. I can't help but wonder if my mother wasn't punished for getting pregnant with me. Everyone I touch gets hurt somehow."

"That's just not true!" Sally said.

"It is so! I feel like a curse! I want to warn people to stay

146

away from me if they don't want some calamity to come their way."

"Oh, you dear child," Tom said, "one thing I am sure of: You are a blessing, not a curse. Whatever else we may not understand, we do know that God loves you, and we love you. You've been a bright spot in all our lives."

Sally went over to Margaret and put her arms around her. "As far as your mother goes, I just have to believe that God has a greater purpose in mind than any of us can understand."

"You know we all have to die sometime," Tom said. "What makes it hard is that loved ones are left behind. For them, God's timetable is never acceptable. It was your grandma and grandpa's time to go, and we had to accept that. It's much harder to accept an untimely death, especially when it comes from the hand of another and isn't from natural causes—as in the case of your friends. It's a tragedy that so many lives were destroyed because of the foolishness of one person. But God has instructed us how we should live. When we cross the line, there are consequences. We can't expect Him to correct our every error for us. Yes, God allowed the accident to happen. But it was Jimmy who caused it with his drinking. You've got to stop blaming God, and yourself. Put the blame where it's due, and then work through the forgiveness. If you can do that, I think you'll get free of your depression."

"Just as I had to forgive the driver of the car that took my folks, you must forgive Jimmy," Sally said. "Your forgiveness may not help him at this point, but it will release you from all this guilt and anger."

Give it up, Heather Lynn. Your bitterness and resentment will do nothing but destroy you.

Heather Lynn didn't say anything. After a while Sally went to her and embraced her. Heather Lynn pulled away and made a hasty retreat from the kitchen. Sally started after her, but then stopped. She returned, folded her hands and stood silently for a few minutes.

Tom broke the silence. "I guess we'll have to keep praying. Maybe she just needs some time to think through what we said. She'll be all right. We just need to be patient and love her."

I hope you're right!

But in the days that followed, it became painfully clear that there was no change. Heather Lynn withdrew even more. Her afternoon visits to Margaret's room had all but stopped. All her time at home was spent in her room. Her attitude stated emphatically, *Stay away! I will not be hurt again!* Margaret felt torn as she watched this girl, whom she loved so dearly, move further and further away.

FIFTEEN

"Y̲OU'RE LOOKING PRETTIER BY THE minute," Althea said. "There, your hair's done. Heather Lynn will be down soon to perk you up with a little makeup. In the meantime, I had better get home and get dressed myself. See you in a little while."

Margaret could hear Althea calling up the stairs to Heather Lynn before she went out the front door.

"I'll be right down as soon as I finish my own makeup," Heather Lynn said.

It was a while before she stepped into her mother's room.

Sally poked her head in. "You better hurry. You have only fifteen minutes before you and Uncle Tom have to leave. You don't want to be late for your own graduation."

"OK, Aunt Sally. I'm all ready except for my dress. That'll only take a minute."

Margaret always enjoyed this special attention from her daughter, which had dropped off significantly in the past year. When Heather Lynn had finished, she held up a mirror so Margaret could see herself.

"Not bad if I say so myself."

Not bad? I look awful. And that's with makeup. It's not too often I see myself, but when I do, it's always a shock.

"Gotta run," Heather Lynn said. She put the mirror down and left the room without kissing her mother good-bye.

I pray you do well!

A few minutes later Margaret could hear Sally giving last-minute instructions as Heather Lynn went out. "We're proud of you!" was the last thing Margaret heard before the screen door slammed shut.

Elizabeth joined her mother. "She seems all right to me," Margaret heard her say. "What's all the concern?"

"She seems fine today. Don't be fooled though—it's all an act because you and Elias are here. This change in attitude won't last long after you're gone."

"Well, at least you'll have the summer to help her before she goes away to college."

"We're not really sure she'll be here for the summer."

"What do you mean?"

Yes, what *do* you mean?

"She's not sure whether she should stay here and work in the pharmacy or go with her Aunt Jessica," Sally said.

Jessica?

"Aunt Jessica? How did this come about?" Elizabeth asked.

"Well, Jessica's been writing her for the past several months. The last letter asked if she'd come and spend the summer with them and help with some of the preliminary work on Hugh's upcoming campaign."

─────────────── CHOICES ───────────────

"You're kidding! Does Aunt Margaret know about this?"

"No, we've been careful not to mention it in front of her until a decision has been made. There's no reason to upset her needlessly."

The doorbell rang.

Not Jessica again! Please, Lord, don't let Jessica get her claws into my daughter. She's confused enough.

Moments later Elias and Sally came into Margaret's room.

"The babysitter's here, and we're ready to roll," Elias said.

It was a perfect day for an outdoor ceremony—just what everyone had hoped for. The temperature was balmy, and a few fluffy clouds dotted the sky.

The Beaumont family sat three rows in back of the graduates' section. Margaret's wheelchair was parked as close as possible to Tom's chair, but she was still in the broad center aisle. From there she had an unobstructed view of the podium.

The band played "Pomp and Circumstance." The procession began. Nancy Green passed by, leaning on a single crutch. Margaret thought of the three classmates who would not share in this occasion.

The principal moved to the podium. "Members of the board of education, faculty, our speaker Dr. Rutherford, parents, friends and, most important, our honored graduates: I welcome you today to this very special graduation. We are joyful because of the accomplishments of our fine graduates, but we are also saddened by the absence of three classmates. We do remember Jimmy Chapman, Lori Braden and Bobby Romano, who died so recently...."

I wonder if Bobby Romano died of his injuries or was

---CHOICES---

terminated. Even one so young wouldn't be spared if his funds ran out.

Margaret's thoughts wandered during the rest of the speech, but she was brought back when she heard Heather Lynn introduced as the salutatorian. She eagerly awaited her daughter's words.

"To my classmates I say, don't look back. Cast off the hindrances of the past. Move forward with new resolve. Don't allow your future to be dictated by old memories that may entangle you and keep you from your destiny. There's an old proverb which says, 'Yesterday's gone. Forget it. Let not thy soul regret it.' Instead, make your own way. Remember, *you* are the only one you have to please. You have the power to do whatever you want to do. Once you've determined your goal, don't let anything stop you from reaching it. You owe it to yourself."

The speech sounded optimistic to everyone but Heather Lynn's family.

"That sounded like a declaration of independence," Margaret heard Sally whisper to Tom.

"Pure hypocrisy, if you ask me," he responded.

All Margaret heard in Heather Lynn's speech was, "I am no longer going to live under your rules. I'll do what I want, and you can't stop me!"

As the graduates received their diplomas, they walked off the platform and presented their mothers with roses. When Heather Lynn's turn came, she kissed her mother stiffly and placed the rose in her lap.

Although Heather Lynn didn't say anything, her thoughts seemed almost audible. "Good-bye, Mother! I'm free at last."

My dear daughter, running away won't help. If you think you're going to protect yourself from further hurt, I have news for you—with all the resentments and anger you're carrying, you're an easy target.

On the way home Heather Lynn announced her decision. "I've decided to go with Aunt Jessica for the summer. I think it'll be a wonderful opportunity to see if politics is something I might want to get into."

A stony silence hung over the car. Finally Tom spoke. His voice was calm, but stern.

"I was afraid you'd do this. Your Aunt Sally and I have discussed this matter and have spent considerable time praying about it. We're not at peace about it, Heather Lynn. We feel it would be much better for you to stay here for the summer."

"I'm going, Uncle Tom."

"Heather Lynn, I'm telling you that it's not in your best interest. If you do go, you go without our blessing." The anger in his voice was increasing.

Heather Lynn's voice betrayed her emotions as well. "I'm eighteen now. I'll make my own decisions, thank you!"

Within the week she was gone.

At the end of the summer she came home for a short visit before going off to college. She was outwardly congenial, but the emotional distance was growing. She seemed like a stranger.

The college Heather Lynn had chosen was only a few hours from Jessica's house. From the conversations she heard over dinner, Margaret gathered that her daughter would be seeing a great deal of her aunt even after she went to school—and that Tom and Sally were not pleased.

Margaret missed Heather Lynn terribly. Even though the times they spent together were strained, the pain of separation was almost unbearable. She lived from holiday to holiday in hope that her daughter would come home. Visits were irregular at best—and lessened as the years passed.

———————CHOICES———————

During Heather Lynn's senior year, there was almost no contact at all. Then a letter arrived, saying that she would be home for Christmas. Elizabeth and Elias would both be there with their families. What a gift this holiday would be!

Heather Lynn arrived two days before Christmas. She seemed more distant than ever.

"Look who's here!" Sally said, her arm around Heather Lynn as she ushered her into Margaret's room.

Oh, sweetheart, it's so good to see you! Her heart leaped for joy at the sight of her daughter.

"Hello, Mom." Heather Lynn bent over and gave Margaret a kiss on the cheek.

"You got here so early," Sally said. "I wasn't expecting to see you until this evening."

"I left last night. I have a friend who lives a few hours away. I took her home and spent the night. I have an appointment later on this afternoon, so I wanted to get in as early as possible."

"Appointment? With whom?" Sally asked.

"I just have to get a few legal odds and ends taken care of. Well now, I better get my bags in."

Heather Lynn left the room without saying another word to Margaret. Sally shrugged her shoulders and followed her niece.

Heather Lynn left the house right after lunch and didn't return until dinnertime. The meal was awkwardly quiet.

After cleaning up the dishes, Sally and Tom transferred Margaret from the wheelchair to her bed. Then they gave her her feeding.

Heather Lynn watched with a somber expression. She sat there long after Tom and Sally left, watching the level of liquid in the plastic bag getting lower and lower.

Margaret, starved for Heather Lynn's company, savored

CHOICES

the pleasure of her daughter's presence.

The bag was empty. Sally poked her head in the door a few minutes later.

"She finished with her dinner yet?"

"Yes, she is," Heather Lynn said. "I don't know how you do it."

"What do you mean?" Sally asked. She detached the tube.

"Nothing." She was quiet again.

"We do it because we love your mother, if that's what you mean."

Heather Lynn didn't reply. She sat in silence until Sally started to leave.

"Aunt Sally," she said. "I think you better get Uncle Tom. I need to talk with the three of you." Her voice was cold and indicated that a grim topic was about to be introduced.

Moments later Sally and Tom stood side by side awaiting Heather Lynn's words.

"I'm sorry I have to do this and ruin your holiday, but I don't...I *can't* fake my way through Christmas," she said. "I've got to tell you about my decision right now."

"What decision, dear?" Sally asked.

Yes, what decision?

Heather Lynn spoke slowly. "Before I say anything, I want you to understand that my mind is made up. I've spent two years coming to this decision. There's no use arguing or trying to persuade me to...to do otherwise."

"What's this all about?" Tom asked.

Heather Lynn swallowed hard. "I've petitioned the court for my mother's release."

Margaret felt an icy hand grip her heart. Sally and Tom were speechless, staring at Heather Lynn in shock.

"I'm twenty-one now, so my mother's welfare is ultimately my responsibility. It's obvious she's not improving. Her condition has put a tremendous emotional and financial drain on the entire family, and we all know...."

"Heather Lynn, we shouldn't be discussing this here. Let's go in the living room." Tom motioned toward the doorway.

"No! If my mother understands anything at all—which I doubt—I want her to hear this. All of it."

Sally moved to Margaret's bedside and took her hand. "We don't see your mother as a burden. We are *committed* to her. Go your way—if you must—and let us worry about your mother."

Heather Lynn shook her head and glared at Sally. "Aunt Sally, I told you. My mind is made up. My decision is not negotiable. Sooner or later the responsibility would fall on me. I appreciate your willingness to keep sacrificing as you have, but deep down inside I think you'll be relieved—though I know you'd never admit it."

"Nonsense!" Tom's voice was heated. "Your decision may not be negotiable, but neither is ours!" He shook his finger in Heather Lynn's face. "I'll fight you, Heather Lynn. We won't—"

"You won't win, Uncle Tom. Legally, the decision is mine to make, not yours."

"What on earth caused you to make such a decision?" Sally asked.

"I'll tell you," Tom said. "It's that sister of mine! Jessica's behind this. She's finally found a way to get back at everyone."

"That's not true," Heather Lynn hurled back. "True, Aunt Jessica stood by me in this decision, and she's been very helpful, but I'm the one who made the decision, not her."

She's blinded you, Heather Lynn. My dear child!

Heather Lynn continued. "Just look at the facts! My mother has lived like a vegetable for the past twenty-two years. She will *never* live a productive life; there is *no* hope. The insurance and public assistance have been cut off. The money it takes to pay for all this equipment and medicine and everything would be better spent elsewhere. Everyone in the family has had to sacrifice a lot just to take care of her. And last, but not least, is the fact that my mother is suffering horribly."

"That's all rubbish," Tom said, disgusted. "It doesn't make any sense. You know she's not in pain."

"How do we know for sure?" Heather Lynn asked. "She couldn't tell us even if she were. Has it ever occurred to you that my mother might have wanted to be released from her miserable existence all along? Even if she were aware of everything, what kind of a life has she had? For all intents and purposes, she's been dead for twenty-two years."

"No! Please, Heather Lynn, don't talk that way," Sally said. "You were always the one who was so sure she understood everything. You always said you had a special rapport even though she couldn't respond. You always—"

"Childhood fantasies! I can see now how I just couldn't accept it when I was a child."

"You still haven't answered my question," Tom said. "I still want to know why you're doing this—you don't need the money, and I find it hard to believe that you're thinking of our welfare in this matter. Why, Heather Lynn? Why are you doing this?"

There was no answer.

"You just can't put your mother to death!" Sally said, her voice shaking.

Heather Lynn got out of the chair and stood at the foot of Margaret's bed. "What do you mean I can't put my mother to death? What's the difference between what I'm doing to

CHOICES

her and what she tried to do to me?"

Oh, no! Not that!

"What on earth are you talking about?" Tom asked.

"Don't play games with me!" she snapped. "Aunt Jessica told me all about it. The only reason I'm alive today is because *she* had an automobile accident on the way to abort me." Heather Lynn stared directly into Margaret's face. "My wonderful mother, whom I loved and adored for all those years, meant to kill me."

"So your motive is...revenge?" Tom said.

Heather Lynn was crying uncontrollably. Tom reached out and placed a hand on her arm. "Heather—"

She pushed his hand away. "Don't touch me! Get away from me! You lied to me, just like the rest."

"I've never lied to you," he said.

Heather Lynn backed up against the wall. "Do you know how foolish I feel? I loved her, and I grew up believing she loved me. I thought she *had* to love me since she decided to have me in spite of her difficult circumstances. I always wanted to do everything I could to show my appreciation for the suffering she went through. Now I find out it was all a sham. She never wanted me. No one ever did."

Oh, Heather Lynn, if you only knew!

"That's not true," Tom said. "We've all loved you from the moment we first set eyes on you. Your grandparents fought for your life, even when the doctors said it put your mother at risk. Yes, your mother had planned an abortion. But if she could talk, I'm sure she'd tell you how much she's regretted it. She's seen what you've become."

Yes, oh yes. Thank you, Tom.

Sally patted Margaret's hand. "I can just feel your mother's heartache. You can't tell me she doesn't understand and doesn't feel. She loves you so much she can hardly bare

158

the pain you're causing her right now."

Heather Lynn moved back to the foot of the bed. Her gaze again locked Margaret's eyes. "I hope you're experiencing some of what I've suffered over the last two years. It's a very interesting situation, isn't it? The tables are turned. You once tried to abort me, and now here I stand about to have your life ended. How does it feel to be lying there helpless, unable to do anything about it?"

Forgive me, Heather Lynn. I love you. You're the best thing that ever happened to me.

"You're just reacting to hurt. Give yourself some time to think about this," Tom begged. "I'll take full responsibility for your mother in the meantime."

"You're not hearing me, Uncle Tom. I said there's no room for negotiation! I better go now. The lawyer will be contacting you sometime after the new year."

Margaret fought to form words in her mouth. She knew this might be the last time she would see Heather Lynn. She wanted more than anything to let her daughter know she was loved. But no sound came from her lips.

"Please," Tom said, "don't go. It's obvious you're upset and confused. You're making irrational decisions based on your emotions. Let us help you."

"Stop it!" the girl yelled and stormed out of the room. Tom and Sally followed after her.

A few minutes later Margaret heard them coming back down the stairs—the arguing continued. Out the back door they went. Then she heard the back door open.

"It's no use," she heard Tom say.

SIXTEEN

Tom WASTED NO TIME GETTING TO THE phone.

"Who are you calling?" Margaret heard Sally ask.

"Joe Haskell. He's a good lawyer. I'm sure he'll have some good advice."

Tom punched in the numbers and waited. "Hello, Joe?... Listen, I'm sorry to bother you at home, but I've got a serious problem."

Tom explained the situation then listened intently as Joe Haskell replied.

Margaret strained to hear Tom's report to Sally when he had hung up.

"So?" Sally asked.

"He says there's nothing we can do until after Christmas. The petition will go to the court. The responsibility for a full investigation will then be given to a committee of professionals, who will review Margaret's case and give their recommendation. Based on that report, the judge will either approve or deny the petition. My office will probably be contacted to provide Margaret's medical records."

"Do we have any say in this?" Sally asked.

"I don't know. Joe wasn't very encouraging. He said our case is unique because the primary care-giver is neither a nursing home nor the petitioner. That may be in our favor since we've shown a continuing willingness to assume responsibility without burdening the petitioner—that is, Heather Lynn. Still, he knows of only one petition denied in this county, and that was because the court determined there wasn't sufficient loss of function to warrant 'release.' We'd be hard-pressed to claim that in Margaret's case."

After a long silence Sally spoke. "I think we should get Margaret ready for bed. This has been a rough day for her."

Tom and Sally entered the room. They worked quickly and quietly as they got her ready for bed. They kissed Margaret good-night.

"Don't worry, Margaret," Tom said. "We'll beat this thing!" He turned out the light and followed Sally down the hall.

There was little joy in the Beaumont household that Christmas. Even though every effort was made for the children's sake, the adults were somber and preoccupied throughout the day.

Sally had just put Margaret to bed on Christmas night and was cleaning up the kitchen when Tom came in. The two spoke softly, but Margaret could hear most of the exchange.

―――――――――――CHOICES―――――

"The grandchildren all in bed?" Sally asked.

"Yes, but this grandpa didn't think he was ever going to get away."

"Are you going to try to call Jessica now?"

"I've got to give it a try. I've been too upset to call before now, but I think I've calmed down. I don't know that it'll do much good. But if there's any chance at all she can change Heather Lynn's mind, I've got to try."

"I'll pray while you make the call," Sally said.

"Pray that I don't lose my temper with her."

Margaret could hear the beeps as Tom punched in the numbers. There was a pause. "Hello, Jessica?" Another wait. "Yes, this is Tom. I thought I'd call you before it gets much later and wish you all a merry Christmas....Yes, we had a wonderful day, and you?" Tom laughed. "Yes, grandchildren do add so much to the holidays."

Margaret could hear Tom clear his throat. His voice was shaky as he continued.

"Say, Jessica, is Heather Lynn with you?...She's not?...Do you have any idea where she is?...Well, when she left here a few days before Christmas, she was pretty upset. I assumed she'd head back your way....No, she didn't mention a boyfriend. You think that's where she might be?"

"Get the phone number," Sally said.

"Jessica, you don't happen to know this guy's number, do you? We're pretty concerned and would like to be sure she's OK....Oh, you don't?...Well, if she does get in touch with you, maybe you could call me....I suppose you know about the termination order....But it *is* your business! Margaret is your sister....Well, I just thought you might be able to talk some sense into her....But....Well....Please, Jessica, just...I'm sorry, but I just don't agree with you....Jessica?....Jessica?"

163

———————CHOICES———————

Tom slammed the phone down.

"Just what you expected," Sally said.

"She said it was totally Heather Lynn's decision, and she wasn't going to get involved."

That's something new for her, Margaret thought. She could see Tom's shadow move across her wall as he paced back and forth in the kitchen.

"She didn't feel it would be right for her to discuss the matter further with me," Tom mimicked. "She hung up. We'll get no help from sister Jessica."

"I'm worried about Heather Lynn. Do you think she's all right?"

"Jessica didn't seem concerned. As far as I know, Heather Lynn could have been standing right next to her."

Sally's shadow projected on the wall as she hugged her husband. "So what are you going to do next?"

"I have an appointment with Joe Haskell tomorrow afternoon. We'll get this worked out."

"I pray so, Tom."

So do I, Margaret thought.

In the weeks that followed Margaret was aware of the many phone calls Tom made and the many meetings he attended. Mounting concern clouded his eyes. Clearly things were not going well.

"It's hard to accept the fact that someone you love can be put to death legally, and you have no control over it," Margaret overheard him saying one evening.

Another time she could hear Tom crying after he hung up the phone.

"It doesn't look too good, does it?" Sally asked.

"Those so-called 'professionals' make it seem like they're doing me some great favor by taking this burden off my hands," he said. "Can't they see that Margaret isn't some object to be casually tossed aside? She's my *sister!*"

It was a crisp January afternoon. The snow-covered ground contrasted sharply with the clear, blue sky.

The Christmas tree was long gone from the bay window. In its place sat Margaret, strapped in her wheelchair. The scent of burning apple wood emanated from the fireplace. Its heat radiated across the room, warming her.

Margaret's attention was riveted to the frantic activity at the bird feeder on the porch railing. A shy cardinal flew away at the approach of a bluejay. Scores of smaller birds flitted here and there on the barren branches of the surrounding shrubs while a nuthatch performed its ritualistic dance on the trunk of a tree.

How I enjoy watching the birds. I wonder how many more times I'll be able to watch them before....

Whoosh. The birds suddenly scattered.

A car with an insignia on the door pulled in the driveway. Margaret strained to identify the crest, but it was out of her line of vision.

It's all over. This is it.

A man in a tan uniform climbed the steps. The doorbell rang.

"Coming!" Sally called from the kitchen.

Don't answer the door, Sally!

Margaret heard the floor in the front hall creak under Sally's feet. "Oh," she gasped as she opened the door.

"Mrs. Beaumont, I'm from the sheriff's office."
"Yes, I know."

In spite of the cold, Sally stepped outside and closed the door behind her. From her position in the bay window, Margaret could see the two conversing.

The deputy left, and Sally came back in the house. There was a ripping sound, a period of silence and then sobbing.

Lord, Sally and I need You right now.

Sally hurried back down the hall to the kitchen.

Beep, beep, beep....

Margaret could hear Sally talking on the phone, but she couldn't make out the conversation.

A second series of beeps followed.

When...when am I to be terminated? Please, tell me. I want to know.

Out of the corner of her eye Margaret could see someone walking briskly toward the house. It was Althea. She didn't bother to knock but walked right in.

"Sally?"
"Oh, Althea, thanks for coming right over."

The footsteps of the two women retreated to the kitchen.

Margaret tried to hear what they were saying, but they were too far away. Occasionally she could hear crying.

Hey, this is about me! How about letting me in on the news?

It wasn't until evening, when Tom returned home, that she was told anything. Sally and Althea had put her in bed but said nothing about the deputy sheriff's visit. Then they went to the living room, skipping dinner entirely. Tom had come in the back door and joined them in the front room.

Tom, please, don't you ignore me too. Won't somebody tell me?

Finally, Margaret could hear Tom's footsteps in the hall, coming toward her room. She braced herself.

He looked exhausted in the dim light. His face was sullen and he made no effort at pleasantries.

Tom, just tell me when.

He moved to the side of Margaret's bed and sat down. "You know the deputy sheriff was here today to deliver the court order."

Yes, I know that. But what I want to know is *when*.

Tom buried his face in his hands for a few seconds. "I'm sorry. None of us knows how to handle this, and I'm certainly not doing a very good job of it."

I know it's hard for you. Just tell me. It's harder not to know.

"The time has been set for two o'clock on Thursday afternoon."

Two more days to live. If I could just speak....

"A court-appointed physician will administer the injection."

Tom got up and paced the room.

"Honestly, Margaret, I've tried everything. We just don't have a legal leg to stand on. Sally and I even talked about running away with you. But we wouldn't get very far with you in this condition."

Oh, Tom, I don't blame you. I know you're doing your best.

"I want you to know that I'm not giving up. I'll fight this thing up to the last minute. Heather Lynn will be back in school by now, so I'm going to try to get in touch with her one more time."

An hour or so later Margaret could hear Tom in the hallway, placing the call to Heather Lynn. He spoke softly, which made it difficult to hear. She could pick out only a few words."

"...Heather Lynn Beaumont in?...Yes, I'll hold.... Can you...when will she be in?...Have her call....Thank...."

"She's not there, eh?" Sally asked.

"Either that or she just doesn't want to talk to me."

Tom entered the kitchen and turned on the light. Soon Margaret heard the water boiling. She guessed he was making a cup of tea and working at the kitchen table as he often did.

Margaret was just falling off to sleep when the telephone jolted her awake.

"Hello?" Tom said expectantly.

There was a long silence.

"Hello...hello?"

The telephone clicked as the receiver was returned to its cradle.

Sally's shadow was cast on Margaret's wall as she entered the kitchen. "Who was it?"

"I don't know. They hung up. I wonder if it was Heather Lynn. The background noises sounded the same as when I called the college before."

About half an hour later the telephone rang again.

"Hello?"

Another long silence.

"Heather Lynn, I know it's you. Please, don't hang up. We're concerned about you. Please talk to me."

Silence.

"Honey, we love you. Please talk to me."

Heather Lynn, talk to him!

"Darn!" Tom slammed down the phone.

"Was it her?" Sally asked from the doorway.

"Yes, but she won't talk to me."

CHOICES

"Tom, I'm really worried about her."

So am I.

"Maybe I should call the college chaplain again tomorrow morning. Maybe he could speak with her, get her to change her mind. If not, and her mother is put to death, she's really going to need counseling."

That's a good idea, Tom. Right now I'm more concerned about Heather Lynn than I am about me.

"I think you should call tonight," Sally said. "Don't wait. It's enough of an emergency that I don't think the chaplain will mind."

"OK. I'll call from upstairs."

Sally came into Margaret's room to check on her one more time. Then the kitchen light went out. Tom and Sally moved upstairs. Margaret lay awake half the night, wondering what was being said on the phone—and praying for her daughter.

Lord, I'm ready to face You. But please help my daughter. Forgive her for what she's done, just as You've forgiven me. She's so confused. Jesus, let her know she's loved.

SEVENTEEN

Tom, Sally and Althea hovered around Margaret all morning. None of them said much. It was obvious that no miracles had resulted from Tom's call to the chaplain.

Two o'clock was fast approaching. Sally and Althea had taken extra pains with her appearance, dressing her in her best dress. Tom had tenderly placed her in her favorite spot—the recliner in front of the double windows.

"I'm sorry." He knelt next to the lounge chair. His eyes were red from crying. "I just don't know what to do."

I understand, Tom. I don't blame you for any of this. You've done more than enough. Thank you, dear brother.

"The doctor will be here soon. Normally you'd be taken to the hospital, but we thought it would be easier on you to stay in your own home. That's one concession the court made,

CHOICES

providing Sally and I are out of the house. The judge was afraid I might cause problems if I stayed."

Thank you, Tom. I don't want to be taken somewhere else. I want to stay here.

"Oh, Margaret, I love you so much. I just don't know what else I can do to stop this madness." He threw his arms around the frail body of his little sister and wept.

Sally came in from the kitchen and hugged them both.

It's all right. You've done everything you could. You both have.

The telephone rang, and Margaret could hear Althea's voice in the kitchen. Her voice was sharp.

"Yes, doctor, I understand. We're not going anywhere. Good-bye."

Althea came to the doorway. "Tom, that was the doctor. He had an emergency and is still at the hospital. He'll be at least another hour and a half."

Tom nodded. Althea left.

"This is the first time I've really wished that Margaret didn't know what's going on," Sally said. "Even though I know we've done everything possible to stop this, I feel so guilty. I keep thinking there must be something we can do that we haven't thought of."

"I've been thinking the same thing. If there *is* something, we better think of it fast," Tom said.

A little less than an hour later Althea returned to the doorway. "Tom, will you come here a minute?"

Tom followed Althea into the kitchen. Margaret's keen ears picked up the conversation.

"There's a car parked down in front of the Petersons' house. It looks like Heather Lynn's."

"You're kidding!"

"No, it looks just like her car—and I'm pretty sure

she's in the driver's seat."

"I've got to see this for myself."

Tom strode down the hall, then back to the kitchen.

"Althea, you're right. What on earth is she doing here? The chaplain said she cried when he tried to talk to her, but she was adamant about her decision. He said she walked out on him."

So that's what happened. Lord Jesus, please help her!

Tom continued. "She's probably gloating right now, thinking the deed has been done. I'd like to drag her in here and force her to watch her mother being murdered."

"No, Tom," Althea said. "That would hurt Margaret more than she already is. Just ignore her and let the good Lord deal with her."

"I know you're right, but I'd still like to see her suffer a little over this."

"She will, Tom. Sooner or later she will."

Tom returned to Margaret's side.

More than half an hour passed before Althea stepped in the doorway. She was crying. "The doctor...just got... here."

Tom took a deep breath and went to meet him.

Althea looked into Margaret's eyes. "I'm going to have to be professional now, girl. I swore I'd never help with anything like this, but I just couldn't leave you with a stranger. I promised I'd behave myself. I just don't know what else to do."

You're doing the right thing, dear friend.

Margaret could hear the kitchen door open and the storm door slam shut. The two men spoke softly.

"Hello, Tom."

"Hello, Jim," Tom said somberly. "I understand you have a paper I have to sign."

─────────────── CHOICES ───────────────

"Yes, you have to identify the patient for me and then sign the paper attesting to identification."

"I'll also want to see your copy of the court order," Tom said.

A long time passed before Margaret heard anything more. Then she heard footsteps approaching. Tom came in, followed by the doctor.

Tom walked over to the recliner and put his hand on Margaret's shoulder. "This...this is Margaret Beaumont," he said, choking on the words.

The doctor held a paper and a pen out to Tom.

"I feel like Judas," he said, scribbling his signature on it.

"The court assured me that you would be leaving," the doctor said.

"We'll leave as soon as we say good-bye to my sister," Tom said hotly.

Tom and Sally bent down to give Margaret one last hug.

I guess this is it. Don't worry. I'm not afraid.

A final kiss.

"We're going down to the church. Believe me—it's not by choice that we're going, but it's the only way they'd let you stay at home," Tom said.

Good-bye, Tom. Good-bye, Sally. We'll meet again.

They left the room, arms around each other. Their footsteps could be heard crossing the kitchen floor, then down the back steps.

Althea didn't say a word. She simply knelt next to the recliner and cradled Margaret's head in her arms as the doctor made the preparations. It seemed like an eternity.

Lord Jesus, I'm totally in Your hands. Just remember my daughter.

The doctor gripped her right arm. She braced herself for the needle.

The slam of the storm door and a woman's voice yelling "Stop! Stop!" broke the moment.

Heather Lynn rushed into the room, her hair disheveled, her eyes red and swollen. She was trembling.

"I...I'm not too late, am I?"

Heather Lynn! Thank God!

"No, you're not, girl!" Althea stretched out her arms. The girl threw herself into the embrace.

"What's going on here?" the doctor asked.

Heather Lynn pulled away from Althea and grabbed the doctor's hand. "Please, put the needle away. You're not going to need it."

Tom and Sally burst into the room.

"Dr. Beaumont, I thought you had gone," the doctor said. "I have instructions to call the sheriff if you cause any trouble."

"We saw Heather Lynn start up the driveway after we pulled out. We decided we'd better turn around and come back," Sally said.

"Look," said the doctor, "I have a court order to give this woman an injection. Unless you have some legal way to get around that order, I'm afraid I'm going to have to do what I came here to do."

"Let me see the court order," Heather Lynn said.

The doctor reached into his pocket. He handed the document to Heather Lynn. She opened it and studied it briefly.

"Here—on the bottom—is the rescind statement which can be signed by the original petitioner in case of a last-minute change of mind. I'm the original petitioner. Where's a pen?"

Tom reached inside his coat pocket and produced a pen. Heather Lynn scrawled her signature on the document and handed it back to the doctor.

Tom hugged his niece. "It couldn't be any more 'last minute,' you know."

"I don't exactly cherish this part of my job anyway," the doctor said, sliding the document back in his pocket. "I just hope you know what you're doing. I wish you well. I'll bill you later." He packed up his bag and left.

"Thank you, Heather Lynn." Sally hugged the girl, and they cried together.

"What changed your mind?" Tom asked.

Heather Lynn pulled away from Sally and turned toward her mother. She moved to her chair, knelt down and took her hand.

"I was pretty messed up when I left here. I figured the best thing to do was go back to Aunt Jessica's for Christmas."

"Then you were there when I called Christmas night," Tom said.

"Yes. But I wasn't sure I wanted to talk to you. And Aunt Jessica didn't think it would be a good idea."

"We were so worried about you," Sally said.

"With good reason. I was an emotional wreck. I told Aunt Jessica my doubts about the termination order."

I bet Jessica loved that.

"She didn't want to hear it. We argued, and I left the next day. I didn't know where to go."

"You mean there's no boyfriend?" Sally asked.

"No. That was Aunt Jessica's invention. Well, anyway, I went to the college and took a cheap motel room until I could get back into the dorm. I've never been so lonely in all my life.

"The more I thought, the more bitter and depressed I got. The guilt was unbearable. I called my lawyer to see how I could stop the termination order if I wanted to. He said I'd have to be here in person to sign the rescind statement—

CHOICES

I couldn't do it over the phone."

"When was that?" Tom asked.

"About a week ago. I haven't had a good night's sleep since. I kept going back and forth—wanting to stop the order because of the guilt I was feeling but wanting to strike out at my mother for hurting me. The anger always won out.

"But I was getting pretty lonely. I realized I had broken ties with all of you when I signed that petition. I couldn't bear the thought of never being able to come home. And I knew I never *would* be able to if I allowed this to happen."

"You weren't just *allowing* it, girl," Althea said. "You were *causing* it."

Heather Lynn looked down. "Yes, you're right."

"Go on," Tom said.

"Whatever has happened, my mother has always been here. She's been kind of an anchor for me. There were times I thought I could hear her thoughts, almost *touch* her love for me. She was my security. I thought about losing that forever. Even if it *was* just my imagination, it really didn't matter."

It wasn't your imagination, Heather Lynn.

"Then Uncle Tom called. I tried twice to call back, but I just couldn't speak. I felt so guilty, and I was sure you hated me. It wasn't until the chaplain told me how concerned you were about *me* that I knew you still cared. We talked about Mother and how hurt I was. We talked about forgiveness, and he asked me if I could find it in my heart to forgive her.

"Chaplain Downey must have thought he completely failed, because I went running out of his office. I needed to be alone to think things out. I knew time was running out, and I had to make a decision I could live with for the rest of my life.

"I was really undecided until last evening. I finally broke

and got down to business with the Lord. Then I knew what I had to do. I packed a bag, jumped in the car and headed here. I thought I had plenty of time, but then I ran into bad weather. The roads were icy, and I had to pull into a truck stop until morning. I kept going in spite of the slippery roads. It's a miracle I didn't have an accident or get arrested. At that point I doubted I had enough time to make it. I prayed so hard!"

"But the doctor was late, thank God!" Sally said.

"When I arrived, everything seemed so quiet. It was past 2:00, so I thought it was all over. I parked down the street, sat in the car and cried. Then I saw the doctor pull in and you two leaving, so I figured it wasn't too late after all. I got in here as fast as I could."

Thank God you did. Thank God you won't have my death on your conscience.

Heather Lynn was crying again. She threw her arms around her mother. "I'm sorry, Mom. Forgive me. Please, forgive me!"

I do, my daughter. I do!

As Heather Lynn looked into her mother's face, she saw a single tear form in the corner of her eye. It traced a thin line down Margaret's pale cheek and dropped onto the pillow.